THE REMAINS

D1484589

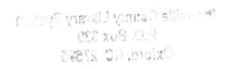

The characters and events portrayed in this book are fictitious. Any similarity to real persons, living or dead, is coincidental and not intended by the author.

Text copyright © 2012 by Vincent Zandri

Published by Thomas & Mercer
P.O. Box 400818
Las Vegas, NV 89140

ISBN-13: 9781612183459
ISBN-10: 161218345X

THE
REMAINS

VINCENT
ZANDRI

THOMAS & MERCER

For Laura, who inspired this story

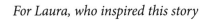

PROLOGUE

March 2008
Green Haven Prison
Stormville, New York

THE GUARD SERGEANT STANDS AT THE BASE OF A FOUR-tiered iron cell block, the angelic orange-red rays of the early morning sun shining down upon him through the top-tier chicken-wire windows.

Cupping his hands around his mouth, he shouts, "Joseph! William! Whalen!"

Inside a dark cell, inmate Whalen inhales his final stale breath inside D-Block. He stands before the vertical bars. So close, the hooked nose on his hairless face and head is nearly pressed up against a single iron bar.

"Cry, cry, cry," he chants quietly to himself. "Cry, cry, cry, you naughty kittens."

An abrupt electric alarm sounds. Metal slams against metal. The noise echoes throughout the concrete and steel prison block. But no one—inmate or screw—notices it. When the barred door crashes open, the shock reverberates inside Whalen's chest. It is the sound of freedom.

"Step forward," shouts the guard sergeant.

Two uniformed corrections officers greet him. They escort him along the gangway, down the four tiers to the first floor.

Having descended the metal stairs to a place called "between gates," Whalen proceeds through a series of barred doors, until he enters Intake/Release.

A female corrections officer stands protected inside the barred window of the small brightly lit cubicle. "Name," she demands, voice detached, but sprinkled with anger.

"Joseph William Whalen," speaks the inmate, not without a smile that exposes gray-brown teeth.

Bobbing her head in silence, the CO turns and locates the prepackaged materials that sit atop her metal desk. Sliding the clear plastic bag through the small opening beneath the bars, she reads off a neatly typed inventory: "One wallet containing ten dollars cash, thirteen cents in coins. One necktie, one ring of keys, one pocket-sized Holy Bible, one black-and-white photo."

Slipping his hand inside the bag, Whalen shuffles around the items until he feels the white-bordered, three-by-five-inch photograph. He pulls it out, examining the faces of two preteen girls. Identical twins. They are smiling, playing for the camera.

"Friends of yours?" The CO, acid in her voice.

"My little kittens," exhales Whalen.

The CO winces, locks onto his wet brown eyes, but quickly looks away.

As the final gate opens, the suited, middle-aged superintendent comes forward to greet the now *former* inmate Whalen.

"Do yourself a favor," the super says. "Keep a low profile in Albany. It won't be a pleasant experience for you. Even after thirty years, people have a way of remembering."

Whalen bows his bald, scarred head, big eyes peering down at the painted concrete floor. "Cry, cry, cry," he murmurs.

"Excuse me?" the super asks. "What's that you said?"

But Whalen falls silent.

Clearing his throat, the superintendent bites down on his tongue. He offers his right hand to the now free man. "Godspeed," he says through clenched teeth.

Taking the super's fleshy hand in his, Whalen gives it a long, slow, loose shake before he makes his way out one final set of metal doors toward the bus ride that will take him north to Albany.

As the door closes back up on the prison, the superintendent glares down at his open hand. His palm is cold, clammy. He wipes the hand off on his pant leg before turning his back on the past, making for the set of metal stairs that lead back up to his office.

"Cry, cry, cry," he finds himself quoting from an old nursery rhyme he knew as a child. "You naughty kittens."

October 2, 2008
Albany, New York

In the deep night, a woman sits at her writing table. Fingering a newly sharpened pencil, she focuses her eyes upon the blank paper and brings the black pencil tip to it.

She begins to write.

Dear Mol,

I've been dreaming about you again. I don't think a night has gone by in the past few weeks when I haven't seen your face. Our face, I should say. The face is always in my head, implanted in my memories. The dream is nothing new. It's thirty years ago again. It's

October. I'm walking close behind you through the tall grass toward the woods. Your hair is loose and long. You're wearing cut-offs, white Keds with the laces untied, and a red T-shirt that says Paul McCartney and Wings on the front. You're walking ahead of me while I try to keep up—though I'm afraid to keep up. Soon we come to the tree line. My heart beating in my throat, we walk into the trees. But then comes a noise—a snapping of twigs and branches. The gaunt face of a man appears. A man who lives in a house in the woods.

Then, just like that, the dream shifts and I see you kneeling beside me inside the dark, empty basement. I hear the sound of your sniffles, smell the wormy raw earth, feel the cold touch of a man's hand. You turn and you look at me with your solid steel eyes. And then I wake up.

We survived the house in the woods together, Mol, and we never told a soul. We just couldn't risk it. Whalen would have come back for us. He would have found us. He would have found Mom and Dad. Even today, I know he surely would have. He would have killed them, Mol. He would have killed us. In just five days, thirty years will have passed. Three entire decades, and I'm still convinced we did the right thing by keeping that afternoon in the woods our secret.

When I see you in my dreams it's like looking in a mirror. The blue eyes, the thick lips, the dirty-blonde hair forever just touching the shoulders. My hair is finally showing signs of gray, Mol. I wonder, do you get gray hair in heaven?

I wonder if Whalen's hair burned off in hell? I wonder if he suffers?

All my love.

Your twin sister,

Rebecca Rose Underhill

Exhaling, Rebecca folds the letter neatly into thirds and slips it into a blank stationary envelope, her initials, RRU, embossed on the label. She runs the flap's bitter, sticky glue over her tongue, seals the envelope, and sets it back down onto the writing table. Once more she picks up the pencil, bringing the now dulled tip to the envelope's face. Addressing it, she writes only a name:

Molly Rose Underhill

The job done, Rebecca smiles sadly. Opening the table drawer, she sets the letter on top of a stack of nine identical letters. One for every year her sister has been gone.

As she closes the drawer, she hears her cell phone softly chime. She opens the phone and sees a new text has been forwarded to her electronic mailbox. She retrieves the message.

Rebecca. Nothing more.

The sender, "Caller Unknown," has a blocked number. Rebecca sets the phone back down on the desk. That's when the wind whistles through the open window.

"Mol," she says, staring out into the darkness. "Mol, is that you?"

THE CITY

Chapter 1

I WAS IN NO MOOD TO ARGUE. EVEN WITH THE ONE person on earth I argued with the most: Robyn, my partner at the Albany Art Center, or what we lovingly referred to as the School of Art.

"What do you mean you can't see the word, Rob? It's right there spelled out in plain English."

Here's the deal: the center's most accomplished artist-in-residence, Francis—autistic by clinical definition, but a genius savant by ours—had completed a brand-new canvas. A colorful, richly textured, postmodern, abstract/traditional landscape that, to me, anyway, contained the word "listen" painted in faint, flesh-colored letters deep within its center. Or, in the vernacular of the job, its *core*.

Maybe the faint word wasn't entirely obvious to the naked eye. Maybe it was difficult to see. But in my mind it was centered and focused enough that the abstract collage of lines and swipes laid out against green-brown grasses and distant forest trees seemed to be painted not over the word, but around it.

L-I-S-T-E-N.

"My eyesight is just as sharp as yours, Bec," Robyn barked. "We graduated the same day, same lousy school, same useless MFA in painting, and I just don't see the word." She abruptly held up her paint-stained hands like a politician about to retract a statement. "Allow me to correct myself. I see the word, all right. That is, I force myself to see it. But it's primarily an abstract rendering, for God's sakes." She tossed Franny a smile. "And a darned good one, too."

"God's sakes," Franny mumbled, his dark eyes rolling around in their sockets like a blind man's.

"Thanks for the backup, Fran," Robyn exclaimed, holding up her hand for the artist to slap her five, which he cautiously did without eye contact. Brushing back long brunette hair, Robyn planted a satisfied smile on her narrow face. "Seems to me our Ms. Underhill needs a refresher course in Painting 101."

"Refresher," Franny repeated solemnly, speaking for no one's ears other than his own. He was seated on a paint-spattered wooden stool before an equally paint-stained easel situated in the far corner of the classroom—far enough away from the other half-dozen private art students who occupied the downtown former Catholic grammar school now turned art center.

The fact that the emotionally distanced man-boy sat for an extended length of time at all was a testament to how absorbed he was in his work. From what his aging mother once told me, getting him to sit still for even thirty seconds at a time at home was a near miracle. Only when Franny finally collapsed into a deep sleep did he become the perfect still-life.

"Earth to Rebecca," Robyn spoke up, crossing her arms. "Are we finished with the 'listen' business, partner? Because I'd like to go home and shower before my date arrives."

Robyn was currently on the market, as they say in the dating world. Since it isn't all that easy meeting men in bars and virtually impossible to meet one while working at the School of Art, she'd become a devoted disciple of Match.com. That is, a true believer in the Match.com dating philosophy of "Mind, Find, Bind"—which, in my loveless world, would more accurately be rendered as "Mind, Find, Bind, *Bail*…"

"Who's the lucky victim tonight?" I posed, sensing a pang of jealousy in my guts.

Robyn grinned. "Allen. Stockbroker. That's all I know. But very cute, judging by the head-shot he posted on the website." Her smile turned foxy sly.

Pulling my eyes away from Franny's painting, I took a glance through the glass doors onto a busy downtown State Street, the sidewalk filled with commuters making their lonely exodus from the city to their suburban McMansions. Now that October had arrived, it was getting dark out earlier. Cooler, too.

"I'll lock up," I offered.

The only artist left in the center was Franny, the others having quietly made their exit while we'd argued over the word not exactly hidden inside Franny's painting.

My partner leaned herself into Franny, planted a peck on his smooth cheek. She then glided across the room, grabbed her black North Face vest from her personal cubby, and headed for the door. "I'll let you know how it goes tonight," she called. "Keep your cell phone by your side."

"Don't call me after eleven," I ordered.

"Get thee a life," she added before springing open the door, nearly pushing it off its hinges.

Just then I caught the image of my face reflected in the wall-mounted mirror above my work table. I looked into my own eyes—the same blue eyes I'd shared with Molly. The same blonde hair, same face. Only difference now was that Molly would forever remain thirty-two-and-under in my mind, while the me in the mirror was looking decidedly paler, thinner, and more tired than a person should at forty-two.

For a fleeting second I wanted to tell Robyn, "Take a good look around you. I've *got* a life." But Robyn was gone and I'm not sure I believed it myself. Neither did Franny, it turns out.

"Get a life," he softly spoke to himself. Strangely, he smiled when he said it. A rare event. He also came close to making eye contact. Something he almost never did. Maybe it was just my intuition knocking on the gray walls of my brain, but I sensed he was doing more than just mimicking Robyn's words. I sensed he was trying to tell me something. Something more than just "Get a life." It felt more like *Wake up! There's something you need to know!*

Or maybe I was looking too far into a deep, dark nothing. Maybe I was just feeling old, passed over, worn out.

I worked up a smile anyway, scratched my forehead with nail-chewed digits. "Yeah, sure, rub it in, Fran," I said. "Isn't it enough that you can paint circles around everyone else in this studio? Including Robyn and me?"

I stood in the middle of the old grade-school classroom floor, waiting for a response. But waiting for a response from Franny was as stupid as it was unrealistic. I'm not sure he even understood a single word I'd just said. Rather, he understood my words, but from what little I knew about his condition, his autism acted like a barrier that could and usually did selectively block out almost anything I said.

I made my way back over to him, stood by his side, and took another look at the new canvas. One last look at the crazy red-and-green Pollock-like squiggles and spatters that surrounded a large field of tall grass and beyond it, a dark wood. To combine the abstract with traditional landscape made for a daring composition, even for the most gifted of painters. But Franny was able to pull it off and then some. Gazing at the painting, I knew that if I were made to interpret the piece for the studio arts course I taught every spring, I would call it a dream. Rather, this is what it looked and felt like to wake up from one of my own dreams—the abstract brain waves somehow combining themselves with a realistic portrait of a field and a forest.

I looked deeper into the painting. The word didn't exactly shoot out at you. You had to look for it, not unlike staring up at a random cloud formation and seeing the shape of a dog or a lion. But I saw it as plainly as the track-lighting mounted to the ceiling. *So why had it been so difficult for Robyn to see?* I might have thought up a sensible answer to the question had it not been for the three quick honks of a pickup truck horn.

Franny's ride, right on time. Consistency was very important to the gifted painter. He was about to head home to his mother's house in the country, not far away from where Molly and I grew up.

The horn sounded again.

Franny jumped up from the stool like a little kid being called for ice cream. But he was no kid. He was a forty-eight-year-old man. He was shorter than my five-feet-five, and far larger in the middle. A regular four-by-four. His roundness seemed to suit him well, however. It gave him this cherubic look that, along with his smooth, red cheeks, made him appear more like a child than a middle-aged man.

I wondered if his condition—his emotional void; the fact that he could block out almost all sensory perception, yet produce such vivid, sensual works of art—somehow made him immune to the aging process. Or did having no real knowledge of aging somehow exempt you from it?

I thought about some of the other, more renowned autistic artists I had studied over the past few years. I thought about Larry Bissonnette and his colorful geometric patterns based on existing cityscapes. I thought of Bissonnette's short, stocky build—a physique similar to Franny's. I thought about Mark Rimland and Roby Park, savants able to capture an existing scene or building or a specific pattern of lines, while at the same time finding it impossible to create them solely from imagination.

If Franny was no different, then might I assume that his newest painting was a reproduction of an existing landscape? Were the abstract squiggles and lines a reproduction of a wild pattern that already existed? If so, where?

Grabbing hold of his tattered portfolio bag covered in fading SpongeBob SquarePants stickers, he took off for the metal and glass door that led to the north parking lot, keeping his baggy blue jeans from falling around his ankles by clutching his belt and hiking the pants way up over his waist.

Before he let himself out, I called out to him. "Franny, what about your painting?"

He stopped and turned. "Your painting, Rebecca," he said, voice low and mumbled, wide eyes planted on the floor.

Although he wouldn't look me in the eye, I swear I saw a hint of a grin forming on his round face. He was about to turn back for the door when I called out to him again. Although I could clearly see where he'd signed the canvas in his distinctive finger-paint F-over-S style, he hadn't mentioned a title. "What do you call it?"

I half expected a mumbled reply. Something spoken out the corner of his mouth, his eyes aimed not at me but the tops of his shoes. He stood stone stiff, portfolio bag hanging over his shoulders, hiding most of his lower body like a portable piece of wall. His cherubic face had lost its pink-on-pale flesh color. It formed neither grin nor frown. With that new, odd, straight face, he laser-beamed a gaze directly into my eyes.

"The painting is called what it says. *Listen.*"

Chapter 2

I DROVE OUT OF THE CITY ALONG ROUTE 9, SOUTH, toward the suburbs. The weather was coming in from across the Hudson River. Light rain sprayed the windshield of my twelve-year-old Volkswagen Cabriolet—the fire-engine–red convertible that had been a gift from Molly just weeks before she died.

I felt unsettled inside my own skin, knowing that on the back seat resided Franny's canvas. He'd never before given me a single piece of his art. I was more than honored, but I couldn't help wondering why he'd chosen this day of this particular week to give it to me.

Since I couldn't possibly answer my own question, I decided to try to think about something else altogether. I tried to think about nothing, focusing my eyes on the broken lines that shot beneath the speeding Cabriolet, stripes like quick brush strokes of vivid yellow.

But I didn't really see them.

Instead I kept thinking of Franny's painting—the large field and the dark woods—and how it somehow reminded me of Molly.

Just ahead of me Molly is walking through the tall grass far behind our parents' farmhouse, toward the thick woods on the field's opposite side. She's wearing cut-offs and a red T-shirt sporting a Paul McCartney and Wings logo on the front, a list of dates for the Wings Over America tour printed on the back. Her blonde hair is bobbing like a pendulum against her shoulders as she walks, just like my own hair.

It's warm. Unusually warm for an early October day. What Trooper Dan calls Indian Summer. Molly is whistling "Band on the Run." She is forever ahead of me, in more ways than one—a happy, carefree, fearless facsimile of myself. The closer we come to the woods on the opposite side of the grassy field, the more my stomach cramps, my heart beats, my pulse soars.

"I don't think we should go any farther, Mol," I say, recalling Trooper Dan's strict rules. And something else, too. There's a man who lives inside these woods. A man who killed some people. People close to him. Or so the legend goes.

But Molly being Molly, she will not be deterred. She will not be any more afraid of Trooper Dan than she will be of stories about a killer who roams the woods. She defiantly holds up her right hand, waves me on the way John Wayne does the cavalry...

But then the daydream suddenly shifts to a hospital room's top floor, the Hospice Center. It's twenty years later. *The hospital room is not a place for healing. In Molly's own words, it is a place for checking out. The room is dark and cool, shades drawn, baby-blue curtains pulled back. Serenity is the order of the day here. The smell is human decay mixed with antiseptic. The walls are covered in dark, faux mahogany. Because dying can take a while, there is a small kitchenette complete with hot-plate and mini-fridge. There's a private bath and a wall-mounted hand-sanitizer dispenser. There's a ceiling-mounted television for passing whatever time Molly has left and, curiously, not a single mirror anywhere inside the room.*

"Stand by your sis," Mol weakly sings to the tune of that old Tammy Wynette song. Somehow, substituting "sis" for "man" has a better ring to it.

I work up a smile, pick up her hand, squeeze it. But not too hard. This same hand was once strong enough to yank a chunk of Patrick Daly's hair out when he stuffed a daddy longlegs down my tank top in the eighth grade. But now the hand is as bony and frail as a bird's wing.

This is my blood womb sister. But that hand, like the twin sister I once knew, is already long gone, even if the portable Siemens-97T heart rate monitor says otherwise. What was once a head of velvety, dirty-blonde hair is now a fuzzy scar-tissued scalp. What were once highly defined cheekbones, pouty lips, and ocean-sized blue eyes have now given in to a steroid-injected face—lips dry, cracked, and thin; eyes the color of old skim milk. For the first time in our existence, Molly and I look nothing alike.

But despite the cancer that ravages her body, my sister sings and waves a defiant fist at Death and the pale horse he rode in on. She'd probably pound a couple of Coronas if only I had the nerve to sneak in a six-pack.

"Stand by your sis…"

Here's what I know from Molly's careful observations: on average, the hospital's hospice floor will lose three flickering souls before the sun sets on this very day alone.

Molly is also full of fun facts about the terminally ill.

Did you know that life-long atheist Carl Sagan spontaneously made the sign of the cross only seconds before exhaling his final breath? Did you know that Winston Churchill drank a half quart of gin and smoked a cigar on his deathbed?

One floor below us is the birthing center, where, coincidentally, Mol and I first slipped into this world some thirty-three years ago. Every time I come here now, she reminds me of this fact, as if in the end is the beginning and in the beginning is the end and all that *great-circle-of-life stuff. I know enough by now to take her seriously; Molly isn't joking. She's still the boss; after all, she's forty-five seconds older than me. Before I leave, she insists that I lay the left side of my head down flat onto the mattress, so close to her I can smell her sour, bottom-of-the-lung-barrel breaths.*

"Can you hear them?" she whispers.

"Hear what, Mol?"

"At night," she says, "when I'm alone, I press my head against the mattress and listen to the cries of the newborn babies."

Then the blast of a horn and the flashing of bright halogen lamps through the pouring rain blinded me like a lost doe. A quick turn of the wheel to the right and Molly's old Cabriolet was back on the right side of a road.

"Drive much?" a snickering Molly asked, her ghost image plainly visible beside me in the shotgun seat.

"Drop dead," I barked. Realizing what I just said, I couldn't help but laugh.

My heart pounded. So rapidly, I considered pulling off onto the soft shoulder. But for now I just wanted to get home, get something to eat, and go to bed early.

"Listen," I heard Franny mumble inside my head.

"Listen for what?" I said aloud.

The word filled my ears with every swipe of the windshield wipers.

Chapter 3

I KNEW IT WAS GOING TO BE A LONG NIGHT FROM THE second I pulled into my apartment building parking lot. I attributed the pessimism to a fire-engine-red Toyota pickup that occupied *my* designated space. Which meant that I would have no choice but to park in the visitor's lot on the opposite side of the common.

It wasn't the occupied parking space that irritated me. It was knowing that the Toyota belonged to my ex-husband, Michael.

I killed the Cabriolet engine and pulled the keys from the ignition. I would have gotten out immediately and braved the rain had my cell not begun to vibrate. I pulled the phone out of my knapsack and flipped it open. A new text had been forwarded to me.

Remember

It struck me as odd. *Remember who, or what, exactly?* Baffled, I shook my head, reading the question—or was it a command?—again and again as if its meaning would somehow reveal itself. But each time I read it, the same, blank outcome.

I searched for a caller ID. A name, a phone number. I found neither.

This wasn't the first time I'd received a text from some out-of-the-blue Unknown Caller. Over the past few months I'd probably received two or three. In each of those, only my name appeared.

Rebecca

It felt more than a little creepy having only your name appear as a text, especially when you had no way of knowing who the sender might be. Maybe Robyn was up to one of her tricks. Playing games with my head purely out of boredom, even if she was getting ready for a date. If that was the case, I was not about to afford her even an ounce of satisfaction by responding to the messages or, for that matter, acknowledging their receipt in the first place.

Except I didn't think it was Robyn. So why not call the cops?

A very strange and irrational part of me could not help but think that maybe, just *maybe*, Molly could be trying to communicate with me. In all my everlasting grief, I could not help but think that maybe she was sending me texts from, well, let's call it the Great Beyond.

As the rain steadily tapped the windshield, I felt myself smiling—happy but sad at the same time. I closed the cell and stared out the windshield onto a brick apartment building. Rain and tears obscured my vision, turning the stately building into something out of a Salvador Dali painting. *Why was I just sitting here? Why did I feel like smiling and crying at the same time?* I needed a minute to breathe, get my act back to something at least close to together before facing Michael.

Remember

"I remember everything, Mol," I whispered as I shifted my eyes up to the Cabriolet's fabric top, as if I could see through it to heaven itself.

Wiping my eyes with the backs of my hands, I exhaled, resolved myself to facing the reality of my ex-husband. I opened the car door, stepped out into the rain. Moving as quickly as possible, I grabbed the knapsack and Franny's canvas. Then, sliding out of the car, I made the mad dash across the green to my first-floor garden apartment.

Chapter 4

I ENTERED THE GROUND-FLOOR APARTMENT BY WAY of the back terrace door. As expected, Michael was seated at an antique wood desk situated up against the living room's far wall. His round, mustached-and-goateed face buried in his laptop, left hand clicking away, right hand raised overhead in the classic gesture of Silence—but which I interpreted as Shut Up!

I set Franny's canvas down, leaning it up against the floor-to-ceiling bookcases to my left. Exhaling with serious attitude, I wiped the rainwater from my face, crossed my arms over my chest, and waited permission to speak.

And waited.

When Michael finally drove down on the Return key with a determined index finger, I knew he'd completed his final sentence of the day. You could almost see the relief pour out of his head like smoke through his ears. He sat back in a black chair that bore my undergrad crest, Providence College, and flexed his muscles as if he'd just gone three rounds with a young Mike Tyson instead of having added a few new pages to his latest opus. He brushed back his thick black hair, then smoothed out his facial hair with his thumb and index finger.

"Plenty hard writing today, Bec," he intoned, baritone voice imitating big Papa Hemingway. "Best work ever, though. Maybe beat up old Shakespeare with these words."

Rolling my eyes, I retreated into the kitchen, grabbed two cans of Pepsi from the fridge, and opened them. I headed back into the living room, setting Michael's soda directly beside his laptop.

He rolled the sleeves up on his thick arms. "Plenty good timing," he said, still in Papa voice, before taking a deep, slow, appreciative drink. "No more biting the nail until tomorrow. Dawn sharp."

Biting the nail…

For anyone not in the literary know, that's Hemingway-speak for writing. Or should I say, the agonizing, all-consuming, existential, winner-take-nothing process of writing. Michael could be so full of Hemingway it made me want to run back out to the Cabriolet, rainstorm and all. The only reason I put up with it was because I knew that taking on the guise of a long-dead hero was Michael's only means of coping with reality. As a teenager, he'd been John Lennon. It had occurred to me on more than one occasion that if he dumped the disguise, he might actually write something truly profound.

But then, who was I to come down on my ex? At least he still worked at his art. I'd all but abandoned any hope I ever had for making it as a world-class painter. Given it up for the lofty position of studio director for the Albany Art Center.

Seating myself on one arm of the couch, I took a small drink and exhaled. "You want to read me something?"

He shook his head and stood up, his five feet, eight inches staring down at me. "Book isn't ready for tasting. Another week of slow, steady nail biting, then maybe."

"Tell me again why I allow you to use my place as a writing studio?"

"You already know the answer to that."

He was right, of course. I knew the answer all too well. The unmentionable truth: since our thirty-six-month marriage had folded, Michael, perpetually and hopelessly unemployed ("Hemingway never took a job!"), had moved back in with his parents. As a result, he felt far more comfortable biting the nail in my two-bedroom apartment.

Why?

Because no way could he write with his retired mother and father hanging over his shoulder, forever asking him, "When are you going to find gainful employment?"

But then, I think there was more to it than that. At the risk of tossing him a compliment, Michael was not a failure as a novelist. His first published detective novel, *The Hounds of Heaven,* had received rave reviews. It was an auspicious start for the young novelist. Problem was, Michael decided that he was now in line for the Pulitzer, which gave him the right to drink and snort away whatever money he made in advances and royalties.

The ultimate result?

An extended bender that had landed him in Key West, passed out on the steps of Hemingway's house. It was then I decided, "Enough is too much." One month in a Poughkeepsie psychiatric care facility, the dissolution of our marriage, and one personal bankruptcy later, Michael went right back to *biting the nail* as though he'd never skipped a beat. While he still imbibed a daily beer or two, his drinking was kept very much in check. Usually by yours truly.

Back to my original question: why did Michael insist on working at my place? Despite his setbacks, he was determined to be a best seller. That meant a return to his roots, going back to what made him a success in the first place—writing in the presence, or proximity, anyway, of me. And even though we were no longer husband and wife, if I could act as some sort of human good luck charm for him, then what harm could it possibly do?

Besides, when Michael was happy, so was I.

"Where'd you get the cool painting?" he asked, the Hemingway guise thankfully abandoned.

I turned, locking my eyes onto the two-by-two canvas leaned up against the bookcase. "Franny gave it to me."

Michael's eyes went wide. "Franny? I thought his stuff sold in the tens of thousands of dollars?"

I nodded. "Strange, isn't it?" I agreed. "He could easily get ten or fifteen thousand for it from some collector down in Chelsea, yet he just gives it to me out of the blue."

Setting his Pepsi down, Michael got up and walked the few steps to the bookcase. He picked the painting up by the borders and, as if it were a mirror, gazed directly into it, studying it at eye level under the light of the stand-up lamp.

"Ten or fifteen grand, huh?" he posed in a scheming voice. "If only writing were that easy. Looks like some kindergartner on a sugar high went to town on somebody's landscape with a set of Sharpies."

That's when it hit me.

Getting up from the couch arm, I set my Pepsi onto the coffee table and stood beside my ex. The painting was positioned between us, below the lamplight, in Michael's hands.

"Can I ask you a question?" I asked him. "Get an honest opinion?"

Although we were standing shoulder to shoulder, I could see that Michael was smiling, obviously pleased that I'd chosen to tap into his cultural and artistic expertise.

"When you look into this piece, when you eye it directly in the center, do you notice anything odd?"

He took a moment to gaze at the painting's center point, alternating between holding the canvas closer to his face and farther away for a more peripheral view.

He bit his bottom lip. "Like I said, some sugared-up, maybe psychotic five-year-old and a Sharpie."

My eyes focused on the bright red, green, and yellow pastel dashes and the pastoral landscape behind them. "You don't see a word spelled out in the center?" I pressed.

"What word?"

I reached out with my index finger and spelled L-I-S-T-E-N.

He bit his bottom lip again, making a funny light-bulb-shining-over-his-head squint.

"You see 'listen,'" he said. "I see S-E-X."

There you have one of the essential differences between Michael and me.

He laughed.

I didn't. "I'm serious. You don't see 'listen' at all?"

"It's not that I don't see it, Bec. Because when you map it out like that, I definitely see the word, or at least something that resembles the word 'listen.'" He paused, chomping down once more on the lip.

"But?" I said, pushing, pressing.

"But I also see the word 'sex.'"

"Michael."

"Hear me out, honey. The point I'm trying to make is that this is the work of an autistic genius who, it pains me to admit, is one hundred times more successful at his art than you and me combined."

The ex was making sense. Beginning to make sense, that is. "Your point?"

"It's like one of those tests the shrinks gave me night and day down in Poughkeepsie. The Horshack test. You know, flashcards with splotches of black ink on them. You're supposed to offer up an immediate interpretation of them, find some meaning, assign some sense to the splotch."

"Rorschach Test," I corrected.

"No duh, Bec. Can't you recognize a *Welcome Back, Kotter* reference when you hear one? Do you know nothing of the classics?"

"You're dating yourself, and what's your point?"

"My point is, I just think that what we have here is the same or at least a similar situation."

I nodded, even though I wanted to tell him that there was nothing subjective about the word I saw in the center of Franny's painting. But then, maybe Michael had a point. Maybe the word I saw was merely my interpretation and my interpretation alone. Robyn hadn't seen it until I'd pointed it out, either. But it wasn't like I had been looking or searching for the word when my eyes first glimpsed the image. Franny hadn't pointed out anything specific to me. I immediately saw the word and since then, I hadn't been able to put it out of my mind.

I turned and went back to the couch.

Michael set the painting back down, resting it gently back up against the bookcase. "Ten grand," he said, a little under his breath—a little *too* under his breath. Then he whispered, "What if we go on eBay—"

"Michael," I spat, cutting him off. "Don't even think about it."

"Just a suggestion," he smirked, eyes wide.

"Here's a suggestion," I said, gripping the empty Pepsi can. "Get a job."

Chapter 5

MICHAEL FACED ME.

"What's up with you, Rebecca? You're wired up tighter than a snare drum. I don't think someone who's sweet and caring enough to lend me the keys to her crib so I can write in peace would be so suddenly concerned with my lack of, ummm, traditional employment. What's really bothering you? Don't clam up on me like you used to do."

I shook my head, ran my hand through my hair as if to say, *Nothing*. But I felt something snap inside my brain. I felt my heart begin to pound and Molly's soft voice filled my head.

"Tell him the truth."

But I couldn't do it. Like a bolt that had rusted over time inside its nut, the secret was too entrenched. Even if I tried to tell Michael, I feared that all I might possibly manage would be to open my mouth with no words coming out. So what did I do instead? I just stared at him, with a frowning, puppy dog face.

"You all right, Bec?" he asked after a beat. But we'd been married, after all. We'd shared intimacy after intimacy. It was true, he loved me, and despite my anger for what had happened during his crazy bingeing period, I still loved him, too. I knew it was obvious to him that I was holding something back. Something that, once revealed, might forever alter the way he perceived me. The way he perceived us. Or what had been us.

I knew how much my silence hurt him. How it had always hurt him when I went through short periods of quiet time. Silence had always been my shield and my sword when it came to combatting the memories of Molly and me alone in the woods all those years ago. Maybe it would have helped if I'd lowered my sword and revealed what happened inside that old house to Michael. But I could never get myself to do it. The secret was too ingrained, too bone deep for me to ever reveal it to anyone. Or was it? Maybe now was the time. Maybe now, after all the years that had passed, the time had finally come for me to trust my secret with someone. Who better than Michael?

Seeking a distraction, I picked up his nearly empty Pepsi can, handed it to him, then made my way back into the kitchen to toss mine into the recycling bin. Outside the double-hung window over the sink, the rain intensified. This storm was definitely going to be an all-nighter.

"You hungry?" I offered, suddenly hoping that Michael would say yes; that maybe after a couple of hours and some hot food in me, I might loosen up that rusted bolt, begin to spill the details of a three-decades-old secret.

He entered the kitchen and tossed the empty can into the blue recycle bin. He wasn't answering my question. Having him next to me in the kitchen made me think about a time when that bin might have been filled with a dozen empty beer bottles and the mortgage was three months overdue.

But then, it also reminded me of something wonderful.

Michael and I, during our first year together, sitting outside the Café Deux Magots in Paris on a bright, cool, early spring afternoon. On one side, the Saint-Germaine-des-Prés church, and on the other, the Seine and the lovers and thinkers slowly walking the cobble walk that bordered its left bank. Both of us dressed in leather jackets and scarves, drinking cappuccinos and smoking cigarettes, our eyes never tiring of looking into each other's faces, our knees touching under the little round table and, on occasion, the tips of our fingers touching, that wonderful electric shock going through our bodies each time it happened. Michael was on his way to becoming a famous novelist and I was going to be a famous artist, and together we were going to be the toast of Paris and New York.

Eight years later, I was standing inside the open refrigerator door of my north Albany apartment. I was looking at the food and thinking that now there was only one person to cook for instead of two.

"What's so important that you can't stay for dinner?" It was a question I posed against my better judgment. Not because I knew what he might say in response. But because I was *afraid* of what he might say.

He pursed his lips.

Here it comes.

He inhaled. "I, uh, have a date," he mumbled, with a quick nervous bob of his head.

So there it was: bang, pow, right smack in the kisser.

I would have gladly cut off my right pinky finger not to appear affected by the news. A lump of lead had lodged itself in my sternum.

"You OK, Bec?" he said yet again. This time with even more concern in his voice.

What I wanted to say was this: Whose home do you use for a studio? Who do you need to be close to in order to be creative?

Instead I planted the fakest smile you ever saw on my face. "I'm fine."

"You sure?" he asked. "'Cause you're acting more than a little weird. The 'listen' stuff and all."

I shook my head and shut the fridge door…a little more forcefully than the actor in me would have preferred. I needed him to leave. But he just stood there, brown eyes beaming into me.

"What are you going to do tonight?"

"Bed early," I said through clenched teeth. "Big class tomorrow."

But if I had said, *Nothing, I have no life*, it would have sent the same exact message.

Michael pecked me on the cheek, then shot out of the kitchen grabbing his leather jacket and beret. "By the way," he said. "What does Franny call the painting?"

"*Listen*," I said, following him around the corner into the living room.

"Come again?" he said. The question gave me pause until I realized Michael thought I had asked him to *listen*.

"That's what Franny calls the painting, *Listen*."

Michael laughed, as though suddenly understanding the punch line to some silly joke. "No kidding," he said. "Now I get it, Bec. You didn't know that before you saw the word in it." I nodded. "Jeez, maybe there's something to your vision after all."

I tossed him another fake smile.

"I hope you don't think me a jerk for dating," Michael said, as he opened the back door and stepped out onto the stone terrace in the rain. "You're free to date, too, you know. Test the waters a little. Who knows, maybe in the end, seeing other people will bring us back together."

I bit down on my bottom lip. "Isn't it pretty to think so?" I Hemingwayed back, closing the door behind him.

Chapter 6

TIME TO BE ALONE WITH MY OLD FRIEND SELF-PITY.

For a moment I thought about taking a long, hot shower, changing into some baggy sweats, popping a movie into the DVD player. Or maybe I would turn on the Food Channel, get a dose of Rachael Ray. Something pretty, peppy, and mindless...anything to distract me from the events of the day.

I thought of just drinking myself into a self-sedating oblivion. But then, poisoning myself over Michael's newfound love life didn't sound very appetizing either. Of course, there was always the cell phone and Robyn. But I couldn't exactly call her while she was on a date.

From across the room I stared at Franny's painting. The word "listen" peered out at me from the center of the canvas like a laughing, heckling hyena.

That's when I got the most incredible nausea in my stomach. It felt as though some invisible creep just sucker-punched me in the gut and now everything I'd eaten and drank all day wanted to come up. Now I definitely knew what I was going to do next.

I sprinted for the bathroom before I threw up on the floor.

Moments later I was back on the couch, nausea no longer an issue. But I felt drained. My forehead was pasty with sweat, my limbs were shaking, my mouth was dry. In my sudden hurry to make it to the bathroom, I must have tipped over a glass of water, because of the puddle that extended from the tabletop onto the hardwood floor below.

That spill became the perfect metaphor for my day. You'd think I might attend to it right away. But Franny's painting was doing its magic. Its *black* magic. It was calling me again. Not only the image of the grass field and dark woods beyond it—a landscape that now was very much mimicking the one of my youth, the field and the woods that Molly and I accessed from outside the back door of our farmhouse—but also the crazy, colorful abstract lines hastily painted over the scene.

To some people, these lines, circles, and squiggles might seem an annoyance or, at the very least, a kind of self-indulgence on the part of the artist. But to me they represented something more. I'd been having more than my fair share of dreams lately. Dreams that involved Molly and me, that involved our walking through the field to the dark woods, despite our father having strictly forbidden us to do so. Those abstract lines made me feel like I was entering into the dream once more, only not in the sleep state. They made me feel like I was dreaming while I was awake. For an added dimension, the word "listen" was buried in the painting's center. A word not everyone saw. Not without my tracing it for them.

Questions flooded me.

Why would Franny decide to give me a painting at all? Especially when the payday for one of his pieces pretty much equaled what I might make in three months working at the Albany Art Center.

Given Franny's autism, he might not have cared the least bit about giving up the money. But then he had never before gifted me one of his paintings. *Did Franny's mother know that he'd slipped me a ten-thousand-dollar present? And why did he call it* Listen *when I was the only person who clearly recognized the word in the first place?* Or so it seemed, judging by the reactions of Robyn and Michael. With the word "listen" being flung all over the place while Robyn and I argued, had Franny made the spontaneous decision to use it as the title of his masterpiece? Or, what was almost too freaky to contemplate, had *Listen* been the title all along?

I pictured Franny's face. I pictured it go from round, rosy, and animated to pale and serious, as if, for a few seconds, the boy-like autism fell aside to reveal the hidden man.

I ran my hands over my face. It surprised me to discover that I was crying. Exactly why was I shedding tears in the solitude of my apartment?

In a way, I'm not sure I wanted to know. But then, the thirty-year anniversary that would arrive on Friday, and all the memories and dreams it conjured up, might have been reason enough for tears. And now this painting from Franny—a painting that was playing with my head and heart.

A tingle erupted in my stomach, along with a dull ache in the center of my brain. I stood up, dizzy. Slowly making my way into the kitchen, I retrieved a wad of paper towels from the cabinet-mounted roller above the sink. Back in the living room, I got to work cleaning up the spilled water.

While I cleaned, I thought about Michael and his date. I wondered how it was going. I thought about Robyn and her date. I thought about Franny, if he was up inside his attic studio painting the rainy evening away. I wondered if he would paint anything else just for me. I prayed to God he would not.

Outside my apartment, the rain fell steadily. *What to do with the rest of my night? Maybe head to the gym for a weight training workout? Maybe head outside for a five-mile run?*

I just didn't have the energy or the will. Besides, it was still raining.

I went to bed without dinner.

Alone.

Chapter 7

THAT NIGHT I DREAMT.

Molly and I come to the edge of the field of tall grass behind our house, the thick, second-growth forest standing like a dark, impenetrable wall only a dozen feet away from us. There is something forbidden and ominous about these woods. So much so that I have difficulty even looking directly into them, as if they have the ability to look directly back into me. I try to focus my attention on Molly's narrow back, her blonde hair that sways from shoulder to shoulder, until she turns to me with that mischievous smile of hers. "Come on, Bec. Let's do it!"

My stomach is tied up in double-knots.

Molly has no fear. Not of the woods, not of what we might find inside them, not of our father, who has forbidden us to ever enter them.

I harbor enough fear for the both of us.

Molly turns, shoots me a smile. She begins to step across the invisible barrier between field and woods.

"Don't!"

But it's too late. She is already entering into a place from which there is no return…

I awoke to the sound of my cell phone vibrating on the night-stand. At the same time, I heard a voice. The cell phone and the voice pulled me out of my dream, away from the open field, away from the danger that lurked there.

"Rebecca." A whispered voice.

In my half-awake, half-asleep state, I heard the deep, raspy, guttural voice of a heavy smoker. In the darkness I lay flat on my back, eyes open wide, gazing onto a black ceiling. Although my heart pounded, my body was paralyzed. I could not move my arms or legs. I could not breathe.

The windows were closed to the rain and the wind. The voice had to have come from inside my head. *How could it possibly have come from anywhere else?*

But it sounded so real, so close. As real as the cell phone. Real enough to wake me. But then, I wasn't awake at all. More like caught in a state somewhere between conscious and out cold.

I lay unable to swallow, unable to move, unable to speak. I felt the urge to pee. But the down comforter had become my protective steel cage. No way could I attempt to get out from under the covers.

The rain came down ever steady outside the window. If only I could have reached out for the nightstand, grabbed the cell, opened it, and heard the voice of Robyn or Michael. The voices might have snapped me out of my trance, saved me from a nightmare too vivid for words. There was nothing I could do.

No choice but to lie on my back and *listen*.

Chapter 8

I WOKE UP EARLIER THAN USUAL. THE RAIN HAD stopped but the sun hadn't fully risen over the Berkshire Mountains to the east. Before crawling out of bed, I reached out for my cell, checking to see who had called in the middle of the night.

I scrolled down to *Missed Calls.*

The last call was from one of my art center students—a nineteen-year-old college freshman and aspiring Picasso by the name of Craig. He'd called me at three fifteen the previous afternoon to tell me he'd have to cancel his tutoring appointment for later that day. In all likelihood, I'd missed his call because Robyn and I were so consumed with arguing over Franny's painting. After that, I hadn't missed any calls. The odd Unknown Caller text I'd received a couple of hours later hadn't constituted a missed call since I'd quite obviously received it.

Remember

So then, how did I go about explaining last night's experience of hearing my cell phone ring and at the same time, hearing a man's voice? No question about it: I had been dreaming. Dreaming in that half-awake, half-asleep state where dreams can be their most vivid. And most frightening.

Dragging myself out of bed, I decided to put the whole night and its nightmare drama out of my mind, greet the brand-new day like I was entering a new life. It's exactly what Molly would suggest I do.

In the kitchen I made the coffee, poured a glass of orange juice, popped a One-A-Day, and ate a small bowl of shredded wheat and skim milk. Taking refuge in my morning routine would help me forget about the immediate past. About paintings that spoke to me. About ambiguous texts. About voices that came to me in my dreams.

As the new sun shined brightly outside the kitchen window, the grass in the common glistened from the rainwater that still clung to the blades. For a quick second or two I gave serious thought to heading into the spare bedroom I'd converted into a painting studio. If I could paint, I could forget about life.

But it had been a while since I'd painted anything. Aside from the occasional ten minutes here, ten minutes there, it had been almost ten years since I'd finished a piece.

The long-dormant impulse was nagging at me, though. So why the hesitation?

While painting could indeed help me forget about things for a while, it could also have the reverse effect: It could actually provoke too much thought. There had been a time when the act of painting or drawing was my sole refuge. My art began for me almost immediately after Molly and I were ambushed in the woods all those years ago. Since we'd been sworn to secrecy, I had to do something to express the torment I felt inside my body, which must have been very much like what Molly would feel when her cancer came for her years later. I covered every bit of wall space in my Brunswick Hills bedroom with landscape watercolors and hand-study sketches, but I couldn't very well produce a large canvas with Whalen's gaunt face plastered on it. My mother and father would surely take notice. What would they say? How would they react to such an awful, ugly face, rendered with such bitter anger with every brush stroke?

But whether it happened consciously or not, I found myself pencil-sketching his face inside the blank margins of the novel *To Kill a Mockingbird*. In the fall of 1978, when Molly and I entered the seventh grade, Harper Lee's story about little Scout, her righteous lawyer father, and the mysteriously frightening Boo Radley had been assigned to us by our English teacher, Mr. Hughto (Mr. Huge-Toe, as Molly dubbed him). While Molly dismissed the story as sentimental slop, it hit home with me.

Why?

Because we had our own Boo Radley living in our midst: the mysterious Francis Scaramuzzi, a man/boy who lived on the neighboring farm and, like the scary Boo himself, never came out of his house. There was also the fact that I lived with the tenacious, gutsy, fearless Molly. In my mind, Molly and Lee's adventurous, precocious Scout were one and the same person. *To Kill a Mockingbird* not only hit home with me, I felt as if Harper Lee had written the story for me and me alone.

I read the book for school, then read it again for myself, again and again. After the attacks, I never let the book leave my side. I began to secretly sketch inside the margins, and when I was away from the book, I sketched on little pieces of white notebook paper and later stuffed them inside the novel's printed pages. Whalen's gaunt face was my sole subject. That cartoon face was a product of both reality *and* imagination. *Had I really taken the time to get a good look at my attacker during those frightening minutes down inside the dirt floor basement of his house in the woods?* I had been too afraid to look closely into his face, into his eyes. Yet I still knew what he looked like. And I could reproduce him, detail for detail.

So what possessed me to compulsively sketch the face? And to do it for my eyes only?

For some unknown reason, it gave me comfort to draw him; to be able to compartmentalize him like that; to be able to control him. Therein lay my refuge in a world where I had no one other than Molly to cry with.

Taking my coffee with me, I opened the back door and stepped out onto the stone terrace. I breathed in the sweet smell of a rain-drenched morning that now warmed itself by the new sun. I would soak in this bright, breezy, cheerful day. Even if it killed me.

For a brief moment I finally succeeded in forgetting about Whalen. I looked out across the expanse of green grass to the large oak trees, the wrought-iron benches and neatly trimmed paths, and the old four-story brick buildings, green ivy running up their sides to the slate roofs. I was a student at Princeton, Yale, or Harvard. Gazing up at the white wispy clouds, I felt like I had become a character in an impressionistic Monet. Maybe *Boats Leaving the Harbor* or, my favorite, *Sunrise*. I sipped the still-too-hot coffee and shivered from the morning chill. Something Monet characters never did.

The white dreamy angels that floated above me…every one of them bore the name Molly.

A second cup of coffee later, I was showered and dressed in my most comfortable Levi's, black Nocona cowboy boots, and black turtleneck sweater. Hair pinned back, I skipped any thought of makeup and instead put on sunglasses to mask tired, wired eyes. Throwing my knapsack over my shoulder, I went to leave the apartment the usual way. Via the back door.

But Franny's painting stopped me cold.

It tugged at me, pulled me in with its invisible tractor beam. I stared down at its many lines and patterns, but still the main focal point came in the form of the word "listen."

Was the painting Franny's way of communicating with me? If it was, what exactly was he trying to tell me? Listen? Listen for what, exactly?

I turned the painting around so that it faced the bookcase. Then I left the apartment for what I prayed would be an uneventful day at work.

Chapter 9

SOMEHOW I KNEW THAT THE DAY WOULD BE anything but uneventful.

Something was happening inside me. I wasn't in any pain. I didn't feel queasy. I didn't have cancer, God willing. I just had this feeling that I was no longer guiding myself—that the events of my life were being guided by circumstances beyond my control. Maybe this explained why, instead of passing by the Saint Pious Roman Catholic Church like I had day in and day out for the past ten years, I acted on impulse: turned into the empty lot, pulled up close to the church doors and killed the engine.

I couldn't honestly admit to being a believer anymore. For reasons I couldn't understand, I opened the door, stepped through the vestibule, walked past the wall-mounted holy water decanter, past the marble baptismal font, past the Christian magazine rack, past the padlocked poor box, and into the big, empty, brick-and-wood church.

The organic smell of smoke and incense hit me. At the same time, I became engulfed in a kind of cold that wasn't freezing, but that somehow managed to penetrate my skin and bones.

I slid into a pew toward the back. For a second I was tempted to kneel, but instead chose to sit. I stared out across the rows of pews before me, focused on the dimly lit altar, the crucified Jesus mounted to the far back wall. The early morning rays that poured in through narrow, parallel stained-glass windows bathed Him in blood red. The place bore a stillness that disturbed me. It was a place not of comfort or sanctuary, but of ghosts. Molly's ghost.

I saw the spot where her casket had been rolled to a stop by the black-clad funeral directors, the place where my broken-down parents stood beside it looking old and so forlorn in their grief. I could almost see the premature death painted on their faces— deaths that touched them both within one year of Molly's. I saw the bone-colored casket like it was still there, still in place. I saw the friends and extended family who came to pay their respects. I heard the organ music and I saw the heavyset, white-robed priest, beads of sweat dripping from his forehead as he blessed the metal casket with holy water.

I saw it all like it happened only moments ago.

For me, it had.

That's when I began to feel like I was being watched. By who or what, I could not say. I begin to perspire, the droplets running down the length of my spine.

Paranoia took over. Paranoia and claustrophobia. I became convinced the big wood doors were about to slam shut on me. I had to get out of that pew, get out of that church—that house of ghosts. Standing, I slid out of the pew, but not without tripping on the kneeler and falling, hard, onto my chest upon the carpeted marble. But I didn't feel any pain as I got back up on my feet and bolted for the vestibule through the wood doors and out into the parking lot.

Standing by the open car door, I inhaled long, slow breaths and exhaled them.

What was happening to me?

Somehow I knew it was a question better left unanswered.

Back in the Cabriolet, I started the engine, threw the gear shift into first, and burned some serious rubber on my way out of the parking lot.

Time to refocus.

Concentrate on the present. Not the past. Not the future. Not on ghosts.

Turning onto Central Avenue in the west end of the city, I decided that I needed to do something to get my mind off myself. Something totally ordinary. Something calming. Do it before I was expected at the School of Art.

No more churches! No more ghosts! No more God!

When the neon sign for the Hollywood Car Wash caught my attention, a voice spoke to me inside my head, told me to turn into the lot, just like it always did on Tuesday mornings. I hung a quick left, pulled into the open bay, set the tires on the tracks, threw the gear shift into neutral and let the machines take control.

Back when I was a kid, the last place on earth I'd have found calm and peace was a car wash. I had a real fear of them. Being inside a car wash felt like being inside the belly of some mechanical beast. The carpet strips that hung down from the ceiling draped the car like live tentacles. Giant rotating bristle-brushes tried to rip through metal, invade the interior along with an onslaught of white, foamy, alien goop.

That was back when I still believed in God.

Naturally, Molly had no trouble going through the car wash when we were kids, the ear-to-ear smile planted on her face making it clear that she actually enjoyed it. Meanwhile, I'd stand alone inside the waiting area, closed off to the soapy Buick and the industrial machine noise by a translucent Plexiglas barrier. I remember following the car and Molly's distorted face all the way along the length of the car wash. From rinse to air-dry to Turtle Wax. I'd still be standing off to the side when the cigarette-smoking, T-shirted men made their quick clean of the interior with their white rags, vacuum cleaners, and bottles of sea-blue spray-on cleaner.

Not much had changed since those days, except that Molly was gone and I now occupied the car's interior alone, feeling the bucking of the machines and the relentless spray of the water against the fabric ceiling. I almost hated for it to end. After all, I no longer believed in monsters, and I appreciated the mechanical utility of machines.

Coming away from the air-dry, I threw the transmission into first and pulled up to the two men who would give the interior a swift cleaning. One teenage boy and a short, slightly stocky white-haired, white-bearded, old man. The old man smiled through all that white hair, asked me to step out of the car ever so briefly while they vacuumed the interior, washed the seats, and cleaned the windshield. In the bay beside me, a well-dressed middle-aged woman who drove a black Mercedes-Benz was all worked up. She couldn't locate her cell phone. She was sure she'd had it on her when she entered the car wash. She hated cell phones. Especially smart phones. Smart phones were dumb, she claimed. She was always losing them. Always forgetting the security code combination so that she didn't even bother to use one anymore. Which made it all the more of a "royal pain in the ass" when she lost a brand-new one. She carried on and on.

A big man in khakis and blue shirt with Hollywood Car Wash stitched on the breast pocket assured her he'd do everything in his power to scour the car for it. It had probably just slid behind the seats; he'd seen it happen "a thousand and one times before.

Make that a thousand and two." But she just made a face and with a dismissive wave of her hand, got back in the car and peeled out, no doubt on her way to purchase a brand-new iPhone. When you're rich, the cost of a new mobile phone is pocket change.

As the two men completed cleaning the interior of the Cabriolet, I felt my jacket pocket for my own cell phone.

Yup, still there. I guess you could never be too careful about such things.

The old man smiled at me once more. He looked into my face for more than a few fleeting seconds, as if he sensed a familiarity. Getting back in the car, I pulled down the window, reached out to hand him a five-dollar tip.

Overgenerous?

Maybe.

But he seemed like such a nice old guy. It made me sad that he had to work at a car wash at his advanced age. He thanked me, asked me to have a nice day in a worn, raspy voice.

I pulled out of the car wash feeling much better about myself. Hanging a quick left, I made my way for downtown and the start of the rest of my life.

Chapter 10

BUT RUSH HOUR TRAFFIC WAS A BEAR.

By the time I stopped off at the Stagecoach Coffee Shop on State Street for a double latte to go, the clock had already reached the back side of nine o'clock. This meant that Robyn would be operating the art center all by her lonesome. Something neither one of us appreciated, since the not-for-profit, art patron–funded organization employed only two people to do all the studio tutoring, gallery event planning, bill paying, public relations, and just about everything required of running an art center.

I got back in the Cabriolet with my coffee, headed for the Broadway parking garage and parked in my designated by-the-month rental space. On my way out of the garage, my cell vibrated. Approaching the congested city sidewalk, I dug out the phone and flipped it open.

The screen indicated another new text. I swallowed something and thumbed the OK button that opened the message.

Remember

That one word, like the last time I'd received it, made no sense to me.

Remember what?

What in God's name was going on?

Per usual, I thumbed the OK button that was supposed to reveal the caller's name and number only to get Unknown Caller.

"Molly," I whispered, purely out of instinct.

I couldn't help it. I was becoming more and more convinced Molly was trying to communicate with me from the dead. Maybe it helped me to imagine her living in heaven—a heaven with cell phone service. But then, what if heaven, of any sort, did not exist? Wasn't that what I believed?

Distracted by the sudden emptiness I felt, not to mention anxiety, I nearly ran into a tall, suited man carrying a black briefcase. "Watch where you're going, young lady," he snapped.

I evil-eyed him as he passed.

"If I knew where I was going," I said, "I wouldn't be here."

Chapter 11

I FINALLY ARRIVED AT THE STUDIO AT A LITTLE PAST nine thirty.

My stomach sank when I saw Franny.

Franny in attendance, the second day in a row. Even though he was the studio's Painter-In-Residence, his visits usually averaged once or twice a month, depending upon his production. Usually he brought in a completed or nearly completed piece, just as he had done yesterday, and we offered him advice on how to improve upon it. This, of course, was all a big joke, since Franny's talent far surpassed our own.

While two gray-haired, retired women worked studiously at their easels on the far side of the brightly lit studio, Franny occupied his favorite corner of honor, round body partially hidden by what looked to be a brand-new canvas.

My beating heart would not let up. Like yesterday's *Listen* canvas, I knew instinctively that this painting had my name written all over it.

Robyn caught sight of me just as I hung up my knapsack inside a wood cubby that had once-upon-a-time housed the little jackets and mittens of long-grown kindergartners.

"Becca honey," she said in an animated, singsong voice. "You are not going to believe this."

I swallowed. Shooting a forced smile from across the room at the two retired women, I reluctantly made my way toward Franny and Robyn. "OK, kids," I said, "keep your pants on."

"OK, kids," Franny chanted while rocking on his stool.

"Wait," Robyn barked, coming around fast from behind the canvas. "Close your eyes, Bec."

"Come on, Rob, I'm not in the mood. I haven't slept—"

"Just do what I say," she demanded. "This is magnificent."

My heart pounded; stomach twisted and turned.

No choice but to play along.

I closed my eyes. But just to make sure I wasn't cheating, Robyn propped herself behind me, masked my eyes with both her hands. From there she led me around to the business side of the canvas, where I stood directly beside Franny. Pressed up against him, actually. As usual, he smelled like he'd just taken a bath in Old Spice. What was also just as usual, was his shrinking away from me. As cuddly as he was, Franny didn't like being touched for very long. Sometimes not at all.

"What you're about to see," Robyn said, "took the master only eight hours of nonstop painting." She pulled her hands away.

When I opened my eyes, it felt like two charcoal pencils were being shoved up into my eyeballs. This painting, as opposed to yesterday's, contained no abstract squiggles and dashes. But very much like yesterday, it depicted a rural landscape. Accordingly, Franny had chosen to paint the piece using sublime colors—greens, browns, soft yellows and oranges, blues, and even ocher.

But it was neither color choice nor style that robbed me of my breath. What shook me up was the field of tall grass. Beyond it I saw a stand of trees that marked the beginning of a thick, dark wood. No question about it, the field and the woods were just like my dream—the recurring dream where I am following Molly. The dream that was not a dream at all, but the re-creation of actual events that took place almost thirty years ago to the day.

There was something else too, something I recognized in the tall grass. The word "see." Maybe you had to really search for the previous day's word, but not this one. To me it was obvious that the letters S-E-E were transposed onto the canvas in the play of yellow sunlight on brown grass. But even with the word that obvious to me, I didn't open my mouth about it. Nor did I mention that the scenery matched that of my dream.

If the word was so obvious, why didn't Robyn say anything about it?

"Earth to Becca," she said, breaking me out of my trance. "Earth, Becca. Earth."

"Earth," Franny said. "Earth."

I pulled my eyes away from the new painting, focused silently upon Robyn's face, her blue eyes. "You're right," I said, half under my breath. "Incredible…for only eight hours of work."

But that's not what made it incredible. What made the painting steal my breath away was that it felt like Franny had somehow managed to paint my dreams. Robyn took a step back from the canvas, squinted. "Whoa, girl," she said. "You're so white, you look like you've just seen your own ghost."

She couldn't have been more right. That's when I once more felt the sudden onslaught of nausea. Sliding myself out from behind Franny's painting, I made a beeline for the bathroom.

Chapter 12

I FLEW INTO THE CERAMIC-TILED BATHROOM, MADE my way for an empty stall, dropped to my knees, buried my face in the toilet. But all I could manage was to purge an acidic mixture of bile and hot latte. Still, my stomach convulsed, my chest heaved, my sternum felt split down the center.

After a time I got back up onto my feet, somewhat dizzy, mouth tasting like turpentine. I made my way to the sink, turned on the cold water, positioned my open mouth under the faucet, and rinsed it out. I then splashed the water onto my face.

My face. Molly's face. As chalky and ghost-white as on the day she died. While the water dripped off my chin into the sink, I breathed careful inhales and exhales. It helped me calm myself a little, but did nothing to end the fear of Whalen I still felt, even after all these years. It did nothing to end the sadness I felt for Molly.

Pulling a handful of paper towels from the wall-mounted dispenser, I thought about heading back to the classroom when the door flew open.

Robyn.

She stood tall, narrow-hipped, cotton T-shirt barely concealing a belly button pierced with a silver hoop. She stuck both hands into the pockets of her low-waist Gap jeans.

"What's the matter with you?" she demanded. "Franny thinks you don't like his painting. And might I remind you that Franny's mother has provided us with one huge annual contribution to pretty much be professional art cheerleaders for her gifted artist-in-residence."

I inhaled again, nodded.

Robyn was right. *What was going on with me?* You just don't walk out on a talent like that, on a sweet human being like that.

"This isn't one of those words-in-the-painting things is it, Bec? Because if it is, I'm calling Albany Psychiatric."

"Phone book's in the bottom desk drawer in the front office," I said, trying my best to work up a smile through all the light-headedness. "Unless of course you want to just cut to the chase and call 9-1-1."

How can she not make out the word "see" in the tall grass? How is it that I see it and she can't unless I spell it out for her?

Robyn pursed her lips, ran an open hand through thick hair. "You wanna talk about it?" Her voice had become calmer, more sympathetic.

Should I be honest with her? Reveal precisely what I saw inside Franny's canvas? The field and the dark woods behind my parents' house, the painting depicting them precisely the way I see them in my dreams? The way I remember them from that long-ago October afternoon? Should I tell her that in the dark and light shadowing of the tall grass blowing in the wind I recognized the letters S-E-E? Should I tell her that Franny's paintings were somehow speaking to me?

Robyn was my friend and partner. Still, intuition told me to shut up about this one. Yesterday's "listen" episode had been enough weirdness for one week.

I shook my head. "It's nothing. I'm just feeling nauseous is all. It'll pass."

Robyn pressed a warm palm against my forehead. "Cold and clammy," she commented, then spoke in the third person. "Is it alive or is it Memorex?"

I had to wonder.

"Maybe you should go home, go back to bed. I can handle things here. It's just Franny and those two rich old ladies who can't paint worth a crap. 'Sides, we're not running any classes this afternoon or tonight." She quickly tucked at the waist, made like she was looking under the stall to make certain one of those same rich old ladies didn't occupy it.

"It'll pass, whatever it is," I repeated while trying to get around her to the door. The former Catholic schoolgirl's room had suddenly become too small for the both of us.

"Wait a minute," she snapped. "Oh my God."

I about-faced, my hand still clutching the door handle. Somehow I sensed what was coming. I could tell by the pensive look on her face.

"You're not…" Instead of finishing the question, she held an open hand out in front of her stomach as if to indicate a growing belly.

"Not a chance," I said. "Way I understand it, you have to engage in sexual activity for that to happen."

"Time to find a man, Bec," Robyn said, with one of her sly smiles and a wink. "Unless of course you're content with your battery-powered boyfriend."

Perfect Robyn: I both wanted to slap her and couldn't keep the smile from my face.

She cocked her head in the direction of the door. "Let's get out of here before the old ladies think we're getting it on." She giggled.

Together we exited the bathroom.

"Don't you want to know?" Robyn said while we were walking the corridor.

"Don't I want to know what?"

We were standing outside the studio door.

"How my date went last night?"

I'd completely forgotten. "How'd your date go last night, Rob?"

She threw me another wink. "I just hope it's not my turn to start feeling nauseous."

Chapter 13

THE REST OF MY DAY PASSED IN A HAZE OF STRANGE and, for the most part, terrible art. Students came, students went. I encouraged them all, answered all questions, calmed their anxieties about failure and inadequacy.

Franny stayed the entire day, busily touching up his latest painting. His ability to paint so fast, so magnificently was beyond my understanding. But it certainly had everything to do with those things an autistic savant possessed and what "normal people" lacked.

All talent aside, I couldn't help but sense that something else was going on here, something that lay far beneath the surface of the paint and the canvas. Franny might have been unable to communicate in the everyday sense of the word, but in my soul I felt that he was trying to communicate with me. The fact that the painting resembled the setting of a recurring dream of mine could not have been entirely coincidental. There had to be an explanation for it. If language and the emotional tools that went with it were closed off to him, then painting had become more than just an art or a vivid method of expression.

It had become his language of choice.

As Tuesday afternoon went from afternoon to dusk, Franny still occupied his stool in the far corner of the studio. I'd made the conscious decision to avoid him. Rather, avoid the new painting. Having assisted and critiqued her last student, Robyn had her jacket on, leather bag strapped around her shoulder. Standing near the exit, she raised her right hand high, pointed it at the exterior door. Sign language for "Mind if I split?"

I didn't mind. Robyn had a life beyond the art center. Still, I couldn't stop my curiosity from getting the best of me.

"Stockbroker?"

She smiled.

Once again the pit in my stomach made its bulky presence known. Was it envy that plagued my insides, or just a simple gastro reaction to my rubbery, half-eaten lunchtime grilled cheese?

"Details," I said. "I want all the juicy details tomorrow."

Rob had her hand on the door. "You want me to see if the stockbroker has a friend?"

"He'll just reject me in the end," I joked.

"Sister Mary Rebecca," Robyn said, as she opened the door. "That's what I'm going to start calling you."

I stuck out my tongue and closed my eyes like a ten-year-old. She burst out in laughter.

I quickly pulled it back in before Franny got wind of the gesture. Not that he'd have any clue what it meant.

"Don't make me scream," Robyn said.

"Now there's a challenge," I said, as she bolted through the exit.

She was hardly out the door when Franny's ride pulled up, those familiar round headlights spotlighting Robyn's voluptuous frame as she tossed a wave at Franny's mom.

"Time to pack it in, Fran," I announced, turning to him.

But he'd already beat me to the punch. In the short time it had taken me to bid farewell to Rob, Franny had managed to seal his paint canisters and jars of turpentine. He'd also packed up everything that needed packing. Except his new painting, that is.

I swallowed something sour. "Fran, don't forget your piece."

"Painted this for you," he mumbled, big brown eyes drilled into the paint-stained vinyl floor tile. What disturbed me more than his giving me yet another painting was his voice again taking on the same odd, new tone I'd heard last night. The tone that revealed the man locked inside the perpetual boy. His face had also taken on the look of a man who knew something I did not.

That voice, that face: they were enough to fill my spine with ice water.

A horn blared.

I nearly jumped through the concrete block wall.

The horn blared again.

Franny's mom was growing impatient. It occurred to me that I should follow him out to the Scaramuzzi pickup truck, pose a few questions to his mother. *Were you aware that he's given me two of his paintings? Did you know that I'm seeing words in the paintings that no one else seems to see unless I point them out first? Did you know that today's painting very much resembles the setting of a recurring dream I've had? That it matches the place where my twin sister and I were attacked by a monster who lived in the woods thirty years ago, almost to the day?*

I wanted to ask her these things and more, but it would've been one hell of a strange conversation for Franny to overhear. Plus, Mrs. Scaramuzzi would think I was a nutcase.

Franny went for the door, his ratty, old, cuffed dungarees dragging along the floor.

Out the corner of my eye, I spotted the new painting resting on the easel. "What do you call it?" I called out.

He turned, slowly, awkwardly, the open glass door pressed up against his stocky shoulder. "The title," he mumbled. "The title. The title."

"*See*," I said, and then swallowed.

No acknowledgement, but I knew then that I had it right.

"Goodnight, Rebecca."

"Goodnight, Franny."

And then the artist was gone.

Chapter 14

THE DARK EVENING HAD BECOME SHROUDED IN A thick, foggy mist. Broadway was empty of motor vehicles, its sidewalks empty of people.

I climbed the parking garage ramp to the second level, where I'd parked the Cabriolet. The concrete garage was brightly lit with sodium lamplight. It was also damp, cold, lonely. I walked with my knapsack hanging off my right shoulder, Franny's *See* painting tucked under my left arm.

My footsteps echoed inside the cavernous garage.

I was all alone.

I didn't like being that alone, the vulnerability that went with it. My body was a live wire, my senses picking up every nuance of sound, movement, and smell. It wasn't as though I were merely being watched. I felt totally naked and exposed.

The Cabriolet could not have been more than seventy or eighty feet away from me, but it might as well have been a mile. That car was my safety zone—four walls and a retractable roof.

I walked, boot heels click-clacking along the concrete.

Then I saw a shadow.

Just up ahead of me, the shadow projected itself onto the floor, as though coming from a man concealing himself behind a concrete column.

I stopped. I opened my mouth to speak. But no words would come.

The shadow moved. It moved backward, forward, shifting position.

At last I found my voice. "Who is it?" It came out as a shout. So loud and adrenalin-charged, I startled myself. "Who's there?" I shouted again, voice echoing inside the concrete garage.

I felt the blood leave my head, sink down my neck, pour down the insides of my body. I felt the blood spill out the bottoms of my feet. Fear blinded me like a black hood pulled over my head. I stumbled, my balance shifting. I'm not sure how long I stood there exposed, body swaying, breathing hard and fast.

I closed my eyes.

And when I opened them, the shadow was gone.

I could only guess that whoever had been behind the column was gone now. That is, if there had been someone there in the first place.

Had I imagined the shadow?

Was my imagination running away with itself?

God, get me out of here.

I made a mad dash for the car, at the same time pulling the keys from my knapsack. I dropped Franny's painting as I thumbed the unlock button on the key face. The car came to life, door locks unlocking, headlights flashing.

I bent to pick up the painting, then ran for the Cabriolet— threw open the driver's-side door, tossed in the bag, tossed in the painting, jumped in behind the wheel and locked the doors. I fumbled with the ignition key, finally managed to slip it into the lock and turn it. Pumping the gas, I turned the engine over until it started with a resounding roar. To my immediate right was the concrete column that had hid whoever had been watching me.

I pulled out of the spot, tires squealing, and made for the exit.

For a quick moment I thought about looking into the rearview mirror, but I resisted the urge.

Better not to see what was behind me, what might have been stalking me.

Chapter 15

I DIDN'T ENTER MY APARTMENT SO MUCH AS EXPLODED through the back door.

The sudden intrusion yanked Michael up out of his chair. "You scared the *crap* out me, Bec!"

I dropped the art bag to the floor, leaned today's *See* painting up against yesterday's *Listen* painting, then made a beeline for the kitchen. I made it back into the living room along with two open bottles of Corona, set one of them down beside Michael's laptop.

"Work's over."

"Yes ma'am." He grabbed hold of the bottle. "Nail officially bitten."

I took a long pull of the beer and felt the cool carbonation against the back of my throat, the magic of the alcohol calming me.

Michael closed his laptop and sat back in his chair. "Explanation."

I stepped back to the *See* painting and held it up for him. "This happened."

Stealing another sip of beer, Michael got up from his desk. He approached the painting with squinty, focused eyes, the fingers on his right hand smoothing out his mustache. After a time, he nodded, cocked his head toward one shoulder, then the other as if to carefully choose his words.

"This is what I see," he said. "I see Franny's version of a rural landscape." He tossed me a glance. "But I'm guessing you're seeing something inside the landscape that I'm not."

I took another drink and bit my bottom lip. "Yes," I said. "And no."

"Which is it, Bec?"

I set the bottom edge of the painting on the counter and pointed to an area of tall grass that appeared to be swaying in the wind. "There's a word in there," I said. "See…S-E-E."

He stood back as though to gain a different perspective. It was not unlike the way someone might look at their own image in a funhouse mirror. He dug into his pocket for his Chap Stick. He uncapped it, ran it across his lips, capped it back up, and returned it to his pocket.

"Ah, Bec, don't you think you're maybe stretching it a little?"

He thought I was bonkers. No two ways about it.

I started to cry.

Setting the *See* canvas back down against the *Listen* canvas, I stormed into the kitchen, pulled a paper towel off the rack, dried my eyes, and blew my nose.

Michael stayed out in the living room. Steering clear of my breakdown, or studying the painting? Certainly the former, hopefully the latter.

After about a minute, he met me in the kitchen and placed his now empty beer bottle in the sink. He moved over to me, looking me in the eye. "In the tall grass," he said. "The rays of sunshine, burning patterns into the grass. You look close enough, you make out the word 'see.' It's not completely obvious, but it's there."

I felt a spark of hope. But then, maybe he was just playing along with me. Making me feel better.

"No kidding," he said. "You have a keen eye. That's your job, after all. I do see it. More clearly than I saw the word 'listen' yesterday."

He leaned into me, wrapping his arms around me. First time in a long time.

"You're not nuts," he said. "But…"

It was one of those ominous dangling "buts."

"But what?"

He released me and looked into my wet face. "We're not married anymore, Bec, but I still love you. Because I love you and still want to be near you, I also know you've been holding out on me." He crossed his arms over his chest, eyes peering down at the floor. "And I'm not talking about this painting stuff, though maybe that's connected to it. Truth is, Bec, I've sensed for a long time that you've been holding out on me."

Drying my eyes again, I bit down on my bottom lip. *Oh God, Mol, what do I do now?*

I wanted her to talk to me, send me a sign, let me know it was OK if I revealed our secret to Michael. For a second or two I waited for my cell phone to chime. But that was stupid. There would be no text messages from heaven. The decision to tell Michael everything would have to come from me and me alone. It had been thirty years since the assault. Thirty years that I—we— had held onto a secret that by now had bored a hole in my heart. Now that secret was consuming me with paranoia, making me nuts.

Molly was gone now.

So were my mother and father.

Who would it hurt if I spilled everything to someone I trusted?

No one.

Not a soul other than those who had already vanished from my life.

My decision made, I looked up at my ex-husband and gave him a glare that might have melted those brown eyes if only they'd been made of ice.

"You'd better plan on staying for dinner tonight."

Chapter 16

A HALF HOUR PASSED. OR HAD IT BEEN HALF THE NIGHT? Only when I had nothing more to reveal did I realize that Michael hadn't touched his beer. It occurred to me that I hadn't touched mine either.

Michael's face wasn't pale. It had turned bedsheet white.

We occupied the living room, he seated on the Providence College desk chair, I on the arm of the couch. Barely three feet separated us. He pressed open his hands against his face, and rubbed them up and down over stubble and white skin as though it would help him absorb the truths about myself, Molly, and a dead man named Joseph William Whalen. Then it occurred to me that he was trying to hide the fact that he was wiping away tears.

"You never told me," he whispered. "All the years we were together. The three years we were married. You never said a single word about it."

For an instant I thought he might try to hold me. Comfort me. But I was glad somehow when he didn't. Instead he fisted his now warm bottle of beer, drank the whole thing down in one swift chug. "What exactly do Franny's paintings have to do with Whalen's attack on you and your sister?"

I stood up from the armrest. I went to the paintings, repositioned them side by side against the bookcase so that they could be viewed together beneath the light from the stand-up lamp.

"At first I didn't make the connection. It just seemed strange to me that I could clearly see the word 'listen' in the center of the first canvas and other people—even Robyn—had to be coaxed into seeing it."

"But the design is an abstract Pollock sort of thing." He wiped his eyes again.

"Not too abstract for me to see through the abstraction," I pointed out.

"In the same way a colorblind person can pick out certain words in a pattern that a person without colorblindness cannot," he suggested. "Or vice-versa. Are you colorblind, Rebecca? I can't imagine being an artist and being colorblind. Sort of a conflict of interests there. So to speak."

I shook my head. "Not that I'm aware of. But then I don't think what's happening has anything to do with colors and how they're put together to make an image."

"So what do you think?"

I swallowed a deep breath, exhaled it. "I think Francis Scaramuzzi is trying to connect directly with my mind."

Chapter 17

IT WAS A BOLD STATEMENT, ADMITTEDLY. AND I'M NOT sure Michael knew how to react to it. He stood stone stiff, eyes wide open, unblinking. He'd gone silent.

"Let me get this straight. You think Franny, this autistic guy, is trying to send you subliminal messages through his work."

"Except there's nothing subliminal about them, at least to me. I can read them just like I can read a stop sign. Even you can read them when pushed."

"Let me ask you a question: When was the last time you had a conversation with Franny that lasted more than a few sentences?"

"That would be never."

"But you think he has the ability to paint secret messages or at least words inside his design of his paintings."

"That's the question, isn't it? Is Franny purposely putting words into those scenes? And if he is, how can he be sure I'll recognize them?"

Michael cocked his head. "Maybe it's something he feels compelled to do. You know, like instinct."

I grabbed my beer and, like Michael before me, took a very long drink. Wiping my mouth with the back of my hand, I said, "This is what I believe: come Friday it'll be thirty years since Molly and

I were abducted. Maybe thirty years bears some larger significance than, say, twenty-nine years, for instance."

"Why?"

"Because for weeks now I've been having these vivid dreams about Molly, Whalen, the attack in the woods, the events leading up to it."

"Vivid dreams." Michael nodded, but I got the feeling I was losing him.

"Yes, vivid dreams. And I also think that somehow Franny, despite his autism, has somehow found a way to turn his emotional disconnectedness around. Whether he's aware of it or not."

"So what are you saying, Bec?"

"I guess what I'm saying is that Franny knows something I don't. He's somehow perceived something. The future maybe. Now the only way he can warn me about it is through these paintings."

Michael shook his head. "Franny has a sixth sense?"

"From what little I know about savants, I know that they use their brains differently than you and me. They're able to tap far deeper into certain wells of talent and yet not at all in others. Thus his unusually gifted talent for painting, for creating images, for putting together colors."

Retrieving his empty beer bottle, Michael went back into the kitchen. He got a Pepsi, popped the top, and came back out into the living room with it. The difference between the new Michael and the old Michael was that now he could stop drinking after one beer.

Scratching his head, he said, "Sounds like science fiction to me. *Asimov's Science Fiction* magazine."

I pointed to the first painting.

"Only a few hours after he gave me this painting, I dreamed of a field with a thick wood on its far side. Molly was walking ahead of me, leading us into the woods that my father forbade us to enter."

"That's no dream," Michael said. "That really happened."

"I was woken up from that dream to the sound of my cell phone ringing. I also thought I heard a voice."

"Now you're scaring me."

"It was his voice. I swear it was Whalen's voice."

"Do you remember Whalen's voice?"

I shook my head. "Maybe not. I don't know. But I knew it was him."

"You must have been dreaming. He's dead, after all. Isn't he?"

"I don't know. I haven't kept track of him the way Molly used to. I preferred to put him out of my mind these past thirty years."

"Then you were, in fact, dreaming."

"Yeah, I guess I must have been dreaming. But then, my eyes were open. I couldn't move. I felt like I was glued to the bed."

Now pointing his index finger at me to further stress his point, he said, "But that doesn't mean you weren't dreaming."

"I agree. It's not unusual to have your eyes open and be caught up in a dream state."

"So who was calling you at that hour?"

"In the morning I checked the phone. There was no record of anyone having called."

Michael smiled. But I knew he wasn't happy about anything. "Then it all must have been a bad dream."

"True, but…" My voice trailed off, as if it had a mind of its own.

"But what, Bec?"

"Then this afternoon Franny gives me another painting. This one matches the scene of my dream—the landscape—almost precisely. He calls it *See* of all things, as if he wants me to *see* what's about to happen."

"Yesterday he wanted you to listen. The squiggly Sharpie lines. Maybe they represent sound waves." He said it half joking, half serious.

I giggled. But it was a nervous giggle. *Sound waves…listen…* Michael had a point.

He crossed his arms, rolled his eyes. I was freaking him out. "What else, Bec?" he pushed. "I know you're not done."

"And tonight, in the parking garage as I was heading for home, I saw the shadow of a man."

"Becca."

Michael was staring at me, shaking his head. Not like he didn't believe me. More like things were moving too fast for him.

My lungs were working overtime, my heart was pounding, and there was a buzzing inside my skull. "There's one more thing," I said. "Over the past few months, I've received more than a few odd texts."

"How odd?"

"Some contained only my name. Rebecca. More recently I started getting the word *remember.*"

"Who sent them?"

"When I try to find out the sender's information, all I get is Unknown Caller."

"Then whoever is doing this knows how to block it. If we had a number, we could cross-reference it on the web for a home address."

It was a moot point. But at least Michael knew everything now. At least I had finally been able to free the secret.

Silence draped over us for what seemed forever. Until my ex-husband escaped into the bathroom and washed his face. When he returned to the living room, some of the color had returned to his cheeks.

"I thought you told me Whalen was dead," he said. "Isn't that what you told me a few minutes ago, when you revealed the secret?"

"I've always *assumed* he was dead. That he died an old man in prison."

"How can you just assume something like that? From what you just told me, he wasn't handed a life sentence. He got thirty years. A thirty-year sentence that just happens to come to end this year."

"He was arrested and convicted in the abduction and attempted rape of an Albany woman. Happened not six months after his attack on me and my twin sister. They put him away forever." I felt a brick lodge itself in my stomach. "At least, that's what I thought at the time. When you're twelve years old, thirty years sounds like a lifetime. A death sentence."

Michael exhaled and once more crossed his arms. "It's been thirty years, Rebecca," he said. "The lifetime is over, death sentence commuted."

The brick in my stomach turned into nausea. "I just haven't thought. I haven't *wanted* to think. You think it's possible Whalen has been released from prison?" I said, voice trembling. "Michael, do you believe he could be alive? That maybe he's stalking me? Texting me? Do you think Franny's hypersensitive brain has somehow picked up on it, and the only way he knows how to warn me is through his paintings?"

He never said a word. Because, just like Franny, I believe he already knew the answer.

Chapter 18

"THERE'S ONE QUICK METHOD TO FIND OUT IF WHALEN is still alive," Michael said. "Google search."

We were standing inside my bedroom just off the kitchen. My heart was pumping wildly. It also felt entirely odd doing something like this with my ex. Doing something this important, this life-altering. This messed up.

While on one hand, I felt about fifty pounds lighter, having been able to talk out the events of thirty years ago, I also felt as though the wooden floor was about to be pulled out from under me. In just a minute or two, I would find out if the man who attacked me and my sister was still alive. If he had been released from prison.

Michael sat at the computer desk in my bedroom with both hands positioned on the keyboard. I watched over his shoulder while he typed in the URL for Google. When it came up he entered, "sexual predators, New York State" into the search box. The search came up with several pages of sites that listed the registry of documented sexual predators, deviants, and offenders, the most prominent of which was www.childsafenetwork.com.

When Michael clicked onto the site, I took an instinctive step back, sat down on the edge of the bed. My heart was thumping so fast I thought I might have a heart attack. I was having trouble breathing, swallowing.

I must've been making distressed sounds, because Michael turned to me in alarm. "We can stop if you want, Rebecca. If you're not ready."

I put my head in my hands, rubbed the feeling back into my face. "What if it's true?" I said. "What if after all these years we find out Whalen is alive? What if he's out of prison?"

"Then at least we know what we're up against," Michael said. "We can defend ourselves if we know what's out there. *I* can defend you. If we choose to ignore it, it might come back to haunt you."

My hands were shaking. Adrenalin poured into my brain so rapidly, it sounded like a brass band warming up inside my head. Michael turned back to the computer screen, then back to me again. I could tell by the look on his face that he was brainstorming. "You never told a soul about what happened in the woods."

I nodded.

"If we find Whalen's name on this list...If we find out he's alive, it won't matter."

Swallowing, I looked into his eyes. "How can it not matter?"

He shook his head. "OK, wrong choice of words. What I'm trying to say is this: Finding his name on the state registry doesn't mean you're in any kind of danger. You never ratted him out; you weren't responsible for sending him to prison. If you're worried about the revenge factor, there's no reason for Whalen to seek you out."

Michael had a point.

Why would Whalen want anything to do with me after all these years? That is, assuming he was alive in the first place. Besides, forty-two-year-old women weren't his style. Adolescent girls and young women, however, were a different story.

I tried to swallow, but I couldn't. On the other hand, I found myself feeling something for my ex-husband that I hadn't felt in quite some time. Trust. I was placing all of my trust and emotions into his care, and I was feeling all right about it. After all, he was the author of a published detective novel, which, in my mind anyway, made him a kind of amateur detective.

"How shall I proceed, Bec?" he said softly, big brown eyes piercing into my own. "It's your call."

By now my breathing had become so shallow I felt like I was about to pass out. At least there was a bed underneath me to catch the fall.

I looked into Michael's face. "Just do it." I swallowed.

He typed the name "Joseph William Whalen" into the Child Safe Network search engine. Then he pressed Enter.

Chapter 19

THE BLACK-AND-WHITE IMAGE OF A MAN APPEARED.
A face. A mug shot.

The black-and-white face of a man who abducted me. Abducted
Molly. Attacked us.

The man was alive.

The monster had been freed.

Michael turned back to me. He started saying something to
me that I did not understand. It sounded like he was talking to me
through a cardboard tube. My legs went weak and the room began
to spin. I sat down hard onto the bed.

"He's alive," I said, mouth tasting like the dried paint at the
bottom of a jar. "The monster is still alive. All this time I thought
he was dead...*wished* him dead." I tried to stand, but I found it
impossible to work up the strength. I began to hyperventilate.

"Take it easy," Michael insisted. "Breathe easy."

I looked at my ex-husband, looked at his eyes. The way he was
biting down on his bottom lip, his nerves betrayed him. I brought
my hands to my face, rubbed my eyes, patted my cheeks. Michael
got up from the desk and went into the kitchen, grabbed me a glass
of tap water, and brought it back in for me.

"Take a sip," he said.

I held the glass two-handed, took a small drink, then handed it back.

"What do we do now?" I exhaled, my breathing beginning to slow.

"I'm not sure what we can do now." He sat back down in front of the computer, set the water glass beside the keyboard. "The good news is that Whalen is registered as a sex offender. That means he's got a probation officer assigned to him by the state and the county. It also means he's a part of the ViCAP database."

The tap water bubbled inside my stomach, made me queasy. I tried to slow my breathing even more. Brushing back my hair with open fingers, I said, "What's ViCAP?"

"It stands for Violent Criminal Apprehension Program. I used their databank as part of the research for *The Hounds of Heaven*. Whalen has to have himself a place of honor in the New York State ViCAP program."

Pausing, he set his hand on my knee. But I pushed it away. I just didn't want anyone touching me right then.

After a beat, Michael asked, "Do you know if Whalen was ever convicted in the actual murder of anyone he abducted?"

I shook my head. "I don't know much about his history, but I don't think he was ever convicted of actual murder. I know Molly believed he was a killer; I remember her talking about it incessantly, even up until the day she died. From what I remember, he was accused of killing a family member or maybe even members. Back when he was a boy. Like I said, Molly knows the story better than I do. Because I chose to simply block him out. Except when I was drawing his face. When I was drawing his face in my copy of *To Kill a Mockingbird*, I wanted to remember him. But then, and only then."

My ex's face had become a mask of intensity. In a strange way, I felt happy for him. He was working the problem—*our* problem—with a sense of purpose. Here was the Michael I loved and missed. I watched him finger a few more keys until the website for ViCAP replaced the Child Safety Network. Using the same two-index-finger style with which he banged out his manuscripts, he typed in Whalen's full name in the space provided.

There it was again: Whalen's face. Not necessarily a bad face to someone who didn't know him. But to me it was the face of a monster—a gaunt, hook-nosed monster. It was also a face I had no trouble recognizing despite the fact that it had aged thirty years.

I looked at the face and this time I did not feel like passing out. This time I stood up, looked over Michael's shoulder, my hands pressed against the chair back for support.

"Sure you should be standing up, Bec?"

But I didn't answer. Instead I studied the short list of vitals that had been stacked beside Whalen's image. Besides his name, the site included his date of birth, October 17, 1949. It also included a whole bunch of what I already knew. That he was small but stocky, white and thin. He was balding now, or bald. But his dark, brown eyes looked the same. So much so that they made my stomach sink even more than it already had.

Under the face was an image-captured date that read, March 3. I pointed to it. "What's this mean?"

"It means that Whalen's image-captured date is only six months ago," he explained. Locking eyes with me over his shoulder, he continued. "I'd imagine they'd shoot him just before releasing him. Which means he's only been out of the joint for six months."

Scrolling down, he came to an area designated Probation Registry. Under the heading County it read: Albany.

"My God, Michael, he lives right in Albany."

"It just means that he lives somewhere inside the county. There's no home address listed here, because even monsters like Whalen have rights. But I can be certain he resides in a halfway house. He's probably allowed out to work, but must report back to home base soon as it's quitting time."

"So what do we do now?" Back to my original question.

Michael exited the page.

In a flash Whalen, or his face anyway, was gone. Somehow I felt relieved. Out of sight, out of my life. But that was just wishful thinking.

"In all honesty, Bec, I'm not sure we can do anything other than watch our backs."

"My back, you mean."

"Your back, yes. It's not like we can go to the police with our concerns. You never reported anything to them. They would just think you're some crazy lady trying to get attention."

He was right. I never reported a thing. Why would the police care about it thirty years after the fact? Especially when I had no real proof that Whalen had approached me in the past few days. Nothing. No real proof that is, other than in my dreams, my imagination.

"I find it hard to believe that after spending thirty years in a max security joint like Green Haven, Whalen would risk his parole by harassing you, or anybody else for that matter."

"Do you really believe that, Michael?"

He cocked his head, squinted his eyes. "It feels good to believe it," he sighed.

My stomach was cramping up again.

Michael shook his head.

"Franny's paintings," he said after a time. "The dream paintings." He was looking not at me but at the opposite wall.

"Yeah," I said. "Where you going with this?"

"In my opinion something, or someone, other than Whalen has you spooked."

"Franny."

Michael nodded. "Humans have five senses: hearing, sight, touch, taste, smell. Franny has already painted you a piece he calls *See* and another he calls *Listen*. It's not unreasonable to assume that over the course of the next three days he's going to give you three more paintings."

I caught my reflection in the body-length dressing mirror that stood on the opposite side of the room. My face looked pale, my eyes painted with worry.

Three more days; three more paintings.

One thing was for certain: if the paintings were Franny's idea of a joke, it wasn't very funny. But this was no joke, because although Franny possessed a keen sense of humor, I felt that he was incapable of doing anything cruel to anyone or anything. Which, in the end, meant one thing and one thing only. "My hunch was correct," I said. "Franny is trying to communicate with me through his art."

Michael didn't share my confidence. Why should he? He didn't know Franny. Had no idea about the autistic savant whom I'd known my entire life. But I could see him giving me the benefit of the doubt. "So he's warning you, giving you a heads-up."

"And to be in tune with the five senses is to be aware of everything happening around you. That includes imminent danger, right?"

"That would be the idea." Shrugging, smiling. "Let's see if he brings you another ten-thousand-dollar gift tomorrow."

Three more days; three more paintings; three more senses; three more warnings.

"You think Franny knows Whalen's out of jail?"

"You might ask him, or his mother, anyway. Or maybe he just senses that Whalen is out of jail."

"I wasn't aware that he even knew of Whalen."

"It's quite possible he knew about him, considering all three of you lived within a few miles from one another."

This situation was getting more bizarre and disturbing the more I learned, the more Michael speculated. I needed not to think about it for a while, if that was at all possible. I simply needed to get away from it.

"Can I make you something to eat, Michael?"

Michael reached out to me with his hands, gently set them onto my shoulders. For a second I thought he might want to kiss me, maybe encourage me to sit back down on the bed with him, lie back on the mattress. But when he looked me directly in the eye and pursed his lips sadly, I knew I couldn't have been more wrong.

"Date?" I surmised.

"Sort of," he said, as if it were possible to have a *sort of* date.

"Same love interest, I presume?"

"Giving it a second round," he said. "But I certainly would not call it love. Not by a long shot." He pursed his lips. "I've known real love only once in my life and this is not it."

I felt my eyebrows rise up at attention at the remark.

Leaving the bedroom, he grabbed his jacket and beret. When he came back in, he said, "Maybe I'd better cancel. I can stay…on the couch."

I shook my head. "It's not nice to cancel on a girl," I said. "You just can't do that."

He stared down at the beret and the worn black leather jacket gripped in his hands. "I'll check in on you later?"

"I'll be all right," I said. "Now that I know where I stand."

He nodded, shifted his gaze back down to his hands. For a moment, I thought he might start to cry. Then he started for the back door. I followed him. When we came to the door, he turned back to me.

"I'm not feeling very good now," he revealed. "I've never seen you so full of worry. I never knew about your past, never knew what you had to hold inside. I look at you, but I don't know you."

"Maybe you've never really seen me before," I said, trying to work up a grin. "Go now. Don't keep Cinderella waiting."

But he just looked at me quizzically as he opened the door. "Promise me you'll lock this when I leave."

As my ex walked off into the darkness of the October evening, I closed the door behind him, dead-bolted it secure. Turning to face my empty apartment, I burst into tears.

Chapter 20

FOR A CHANGE IT HAD BEEN A NIGHT WITHOUT dreams, a night without voices, a night without texts. But then it had also been a night of sleeplessness. Or, when I did manage to sleep at all, I would wake up minutes later with a start, as if to sleep even for a minute was to let my guard down. My mind and my body were speaking to me, telling me I had to start getting to the bottom of the reasons behind Franny's paintings. It meant that instead of going straight to work, I would go see Franny's mother, face-to-face.

I called Robyn from the car just as I was crossing the Hudson River via the South Troy Bridge. I told her I'd be in sometime later that morning after I took care of some personal business. She told me, "No sweat." That she owed me for all those nights I closed up alone. "Take the freaking *day*, Bec," she insisted.

I told her I wouldn't know what to freaking do with myself.

Ten minutes later I entered into what Michael referred to as Indian Country. This was the rural landscape of Brunswick Hills and beyond that, the foothills that eventually turned into the blue mountains of Massachusetts. I cruised US Rural Route 2 that paralleled the winding path of the Postenkill, a stream as wide and deep in parts as a river. It always ran fast and frothy white in early October from the September rains that soaked the region. Trooper

Dan taught us to fish for trout in the stream, back when we were twin pups. While I never caught much of anything (the only thing I hated more than touching a live fish was touching a worm), Molly never made it home without a fish or two in her creel (she loved the feel of live fish *and* worms). Her fishing prowess made our dad proud, especially in light of my, ah, *girlish* apprehension. I've sometimes wondered if Molly might have been the boy Dad never had.

After a while I made it through the small town of Poestenkill with its two or three antique shops, general store, and one-bay firehouse. From there I continued along Route 2 until I came to Garfield Road, where I hooked a sharp right at the Civil War cemetery.

It had been a long time since I'd made a trek back to this country and I felt the years piling up in my stomach like so many bricks. Ten bricks—one for every year I'd been away. Ten years that dated back to Molly's death. It's not that I made a conscious decision never to return. It's just that there was nothing left for me here. Nothing other than the shell of a house that had been handed down to me by my parents upon their deaths, along with the land that went with it, including a major chunk of Mount Desolation.

I hadn't been entirely neglectful.

I paid the taxes on the property, even paid a local jack-of-all-trades to keep the house up and to mow the field grass. But since Molly passed on, I hadn't been able to get myself to return to the old homestead, as if some invisible force field was holding me back—the never-too-distant memory of a monster who once lurked inside the deep woods. Not even Michael, my former husband, had laid eyes on the place.

So why then, after all this time, had I come back to the Brunswick Hills?

Francis Scaramuzzi and his mother had been my neighbors, which in this unspoiled country meant that our respective spreads were located a good three miles from one another. Out of sight but not out of mind.

The sun was shining bright as I pulled into the driveway of Franny's two-story white clapboard farmhouse. I cut the engine on the Cabriolet, got out. Immediately I was struck by the smell of the land, of the century-old trees that surrounded me, their leaves golden and shedding in the fall breeze.

Just like my parents' place, the Scaramuzzi farm no longer supported any livestock or animals. But the barn and the fields beyond it were still there. The fields of tall grass seemed to go on forever, though they actually touched the foothills just a mile eastward.

I made my way up the gravel drive onto the porch, reached for the doorbell. But before I could press it, I heard a car pulling up behind me onto the gravel drive.

Caroline. Franny's mom.

She drove a blue Chevy pickup that had to be ten years older than me and that still looked to be in tip-top shape. Stenciled on both the driver's and passenger's side doors were the words "Scaramuzzi Farms" on behalf of the vegetable-slash-art stand that Mrs. Scaramuzzi used to set up on the front lawn from spring to late fall. The art part of the enterprise came about when Franny started selling his original oil paintings alongside the ears of corn, potatoes, tomatoes, pumpkins, cucumbers, and summer squash, plus homemade apple and blueberry pies.

Now that he could regularly command five figures or more for his work, Franny no longer had to hawk it out of a three-sided shack on the front lawn. It also meant his mother no longer had to make ends meet by selling homegrown vegetables and baked goods.

Planting a smile, albeit a nervous one, on my face, I watched the small but still athletic woman exit the truck, slam the door closed with a vigor that belied her seventy-plus years. As she made her way up the drive I was able to make out her smiling, smooth face, her brown eyes and friendly mouth.

She was wearing a red bandanna over long, thick, salt-and-pepper hair. Silver earrings dangled from her earlobes. She wore an eggshell-colored turtleneck over a pair of well-worn Levi's and, for shoes, a pair of green Crocs over gray wool socks.

She stopped upon reaching the porch steps. "Something's wrong with this scenario, young lady," she said with a smile. "I dropped Franny off at the art center a while ago. Aren't you supposed to be critiquing him right about now?"

I laughed. "Come on, Mrs. S," I said, "you know as well as I do that Franny critiques us."

Laughing, she turned away, as if the comment made her blush, even though it had been directed at her son.

"'Sides," I said, "Robyn has been begging me to get some one-on-one face time with our most gifted artist-in-residence."

"Don't forget famous," Mrs. S said.

I raised my eyebrows while she made the stairs, walked on past me, and opened the unlocked door.

"Just yesterday," she went on speaking as we entered the house, "I got a call from New York. An associate producer from MSNBC, grew up in this area."

"Why does that not surprise me?" I said, moving into the semidark, musty-smelling living room.

"Woman by the name of…" She peered upward as if her memory escaped her. And apparently it had. "Oh I forget her name. But she had a nice voice and she was all excited about Franny, his art. She's putting together a prime time special report on autistic savants. Musical savants, mathematical, literary. Franny would cover the visual arts aspect."

She headed through the living room and into the kitchen at the end of it. When I entered behind her, I watched her take a teakettle from off the gas stove and begin filling it with water from the tap. The spacious kitchen was like something out of *Town & Country* Magazine. Quaint, comfortable, cozy.

"So don't leave me in the dark, Mrs. S. Did you accept the producer's offer?"

"I haven't called back," she admitted solemnly. "To be honest, I have not made up my mind about it."

"It could mean fame and fortune for Franny," I said, stating the obvious. "A spot on MSNBC in the prime time would really catapult him into the limelight."

"Which is exactly what worries me, Rebecca." She sighed as she joined me at the large harvest table. "It's just that Franny has never been beyond the farm. Oh, he goes to Albany, of course. To the art center. But I just can't imagine how he might handle going on national television in New York City. I…" She let the thought trail off while shaking her head, staring down at the tabletop.

Her gestures, her ambivalence: they made me wonder who was more scared of Franny's moving on, this lovely widow or Franny himself.

There was a long pause. Long enough for it to become a little uncomfortable. When the teakettle whistle blew, it nearly frightened me out of my chair. Mrs. Scaramuzzi got up.

"Enough television talk," she ordered. "Obviously you've made a prodigal return to your homeland to meet with me up close and personal. So let's get to it." Grabbing hold of the teakettle, she set it onto an unlit burner. "But before we get started," she went on, "I'd like it if you'd call me Caroline. Mrs. Scaramuzzi was my husband's mother."

I laughed. "Caroline," I said, trying it on for size. "Caroline is fine."

I got up from the table to help her with the tea. While Caroline set out mugs with good old-fashioned Salada tea bags in them, I picked up the kettle and began pouring in the hot water.

"Go sit, Caroline," I insisted. "I'll get this."

"A guest in my own home," she said, sitting back down at the table. "Feels kind of sweet."

"How do you take your tea?" I asked, while replacing the kettle onto the stove.

"Naked," she said. "Like my men."

The ice broken, we both had a good laugh while I carried the mugs back over to the table.

Chapter 21

EVEN THOUGH THE SCARAMUZZI FARMHOUSE HAD to be over a century old, most of the stainless-steel appliances inside the kitchen were new, no doubt the spoils of Franny's hard work and talent. You couldn't look at a single wall without spotting at least one reminder of the autistic savant's success over the many years I'd known of him, and the seven years I'd truly come to know him while working at the art center.

Even inside the kitchen, the walls and shelves were ripe with framed sketches, limited prints, original canvases of every type, style, and theme. From crazy, eye-dancing abstracts to serene landscapes, to black-and-white self-portraits to pencil sketch studies of his mother cooking, pinning laundry to the outside line, working in the vegetable garden.

The one image that provoked skin-deep chills was a simple drawing of Caroline. She was standing alone at the edge of the gravel drive, long hair blowing back across her face by a storm-driven wind produced by blue-black clouds visible on the horizon. It was a scene that evoked Wyeth, but that hit me deep inside since its true-life subject was sitting directly in front of me.

We sat with our steaming mugs of tea. I attempted to sip mine. But it was still too hot.

Caroline smiled graciously. "So what's on your mind, young lady?"

I guess when you've lived more than seventy years, forty-two seems almost adolescent.

"Are you aware that over the past two days Franny's given me two of his paintings?"

I looked for a sign of surprise on her face. An upturned brow, a flushing of the cheeks. I got neither as she calmly sipped her tea.

"I'm aware that Franny has been working feverishly. I see that he brings his paintings along with him to the art center. But I didn't know he was painting them for you, Rebecca." She peered down at her tea, then up at me again. "Why do you think he would do that?"

"That's what I came here to find out. So far this week he's been at the studio every day, all day. He's there right now with Robyn."

"That's right."

"Today will make the third day in a row. A record for him. And did he take another painting with him today?"

My stomach did a little flip when she nodded. I couldn't imagine what kind of image I would have to confront when I made my return to the studio later that morning. *What word might I see buried inside it? Which one of the three out of five senses left?*

"If Francis wants to give you his paintings," Caroline said after a time, "then that's his business. I have no problem with it."

"Oh don't get me wrong, I love Franny and I'm honored to be gifted his work. To be frank, I've learned from his style."

Caroline shook her head, pursed her lips. "Then what's the problem?"

I took another sip of my still-too-hot tea. "Has Franny been acting a little...strange lately?"

Caroline broke out in laughter. "He's autistic, Rebecca." She giggled. "He's *always* acting strangely."

I was more than a little taken aback at her response. And I think she knew it. Because she started laughing even harder, from deep inside the raspy lungs of a former smoker.

"It's a joke," she said, eyes wide. "An autistic boy, strange? When you stand in my shoes, young lady, you don't expect normalcy from a boy like Francis. You expect something new and weird and quite wonderful with each new day."

I took notice of her referring to a man pushing fifty as a boy. But then, Franny *was* a boy. He would never grow old, despite his body.

"Listen Rebecca," she said, "I can tell something's got you upset, so perhaps I should explain a little about Francis's condition. It might shed some light, help you to understand why he does the things he does—why he paints the way he does."

I nodded. It was worth a shot.

She sat back, both hands wrapped around her mug, deep eyes peering into it as though it were a crystal ball that revealed the past instead of the future. "Not long after Franny was born, he was diagnosed with retardation," she said in an exasperated tone. "That sounds harsh today, and I can't begin to tell you how devastating it sounded almost a half century ago, even though that awful word was common then."

"They couldn't tell he was autistic?"

"They didn't know what autism was. Back then, it was often confused with insanity. The most my husband and I could expect for Francis was for him to perhaps live a relatively comfortable existence inside a facility—or what they used to refer to as an *asylum,* back in the day. But that would have been a disaster. Autism was only one of his problems. He was also affected by heart and lung problems. Congenital ailments that still plague him and force the daily intake of blood thinners." She paused, eyes still focused on her tea. "In all honesty, Rebecca, Franny is not long for this world."

Her revelation hit me like a punch to the belly. Franny had always seemed so healthy to me. I also could not imagine a world without him.

"In any case," she said, "I—*we*—resolved to raise Francis here, on the farm. Give him as normal a life as possible, for as long as his life lasted." Finally she raised her face and looked me directly in the eye. "And thank God we did. Because it didn't take long for us to discover that the doctors had been all wrong."

I wasn't sure I understood her, so I asked her to explain.

She got up from out of her chair. "Come on," she said. "I've got something to show you."

I stood up, began to follow her. "What exactly did the doctors have wrong?" I asked while being led to an old door at the far side of the kitchen.

She brushed back her long hair, opened the door to reveal a dark basement. Tugging on the string that ignited an exposed overhead lightbulb, she said, "Francis might have been different, but he was far from retarded. Down in this basement is the evidence."

She wiped away a spiderweb and began to climb down the old wood plank stairs.

Ever the cautious twin sister, I followed.

Chapter 22

WITH ITS EXPOSED DAMP DIRT FLOOR SURROUNDED by fieldstone foundation walls, the basement felt more like a cave than the foundation for an old farmhouse. A single overhead lightbulb sprayed a dull beam on the gray-brown dirt. The smell of old raw onions and mold permeated the moist air. Caroline led me across the length of the open floor to a large closet-like room that had been built out of plywood, its walls covered with clear plastic over Styrofoam boards. Protruding from the side of the room was a long section of rubbery ductwork that snaked itself all the way up to an opening at the top of the foundation wall.

This was a room built *inside* a room—a space independent from the house that contained it, and that maintained its own ventilation system. As an artist, I wasn't ignorant of such specialty rooms. Lots of artists and art collectors had them built inside their homes and galleries in order to better preserve their precious treasures. Because after all, properly maintained art never decreases in value, no matter what.

When Caroline opened the door to the room, I could immediately see that she possessed quite the collection. The brightly lit space was stacked full with original art pieces. Every bit of wall space in a room I estimated to be twelve by twelve feet was covered with paintings, sketches, and black-and-white drawings, the largest of which was a full-sized self-portrait of Franny himself. The artist was dressed in his usual uniform of baggy jeans, Converse high-tops, and a fire-engine-red T-shirt. In the painting, his face was noticeably younger, but just as round, just as smooth and chubby. His hair was thicker but mussed up. Thin arms hung down straight at his side, almost like a toy soldier standing at attention.

The expression on his face was nothing less than stunning. The piercing gray eyes cut holes in my chest. The image seemed so real to me, so lifelike and vivid, I half expected him to open up his mouth and speak.

Caroline must have taken notice of my amazement. "Francis painted that ten years ago," she explained, breaking me out of my spell. "Some of these paintings he did at as early as three years old."

That's when she reached out, took hold of my hand, and led me to a small, postcard-sized pastel drawing of a hobby horse. Its execution was at once as detailed and photographically rendered as a *Saturday Evening Post* Rockwell and as distorted, distant, and disturbing as a van Gogh.

"He was *three*?"

"Three," she said. "It was an exciting time for us. Because we knew then for certain that Franny was no idiot. He was *gifted*."

"The G word," I said. "I don't use it often. Never at the art center. Except for *one* very special artist."

Caroline bit down on her bottom lip, nodded. "Tell me something, Rebecca, how much do you know about Autistic Savant Syndrome?"

I shook my head, breathed in the room's strong scent of paint, turpentine, and alcohol. "Other than what I've learned from my contact with Franny over the years, not a whole lot."

Crossing her arms, Caroline focused her eyes not on me, but on the eclectic pieces of art that covered the wall behind me.

"In layman's terms," she went on, "people with autism are born with miswired neurons. In a few scattered cases, this affords them extraordinary gifts." She raised her hands as if to say, *Just take a good look around at all these gifts.* "Not long before Francis painted that hobby horse, we were told that he would never be cured. Francis would never be mainstreamed and would, for the duration of his life, require constant care."

I looked over her shoulder at Franny's face, looked into eyes that seemed to lock on mine from wherever I stood inside the small room. "Not the most optimistic of outlooks."

"Until he started drawing and painting," she said. "That's when everything changed."

"When exactly did he start?"

"He was three years old when he started sketching. Maybe the boy couldn't communicate with us the way we wanted him to. Maybe he couldn't stand loud noises or closed-in spaces. Maybe he couldn't look us straight in the eyes. But one day in his third year, he picks up a pencil and paper, he starts to draw like an artist three times his age. My husband and I were floored, to say the least.

"We showed his drawings and sketches to his doctors at the Parsons Center in Albany. They in turn found them remarkable and immediately labeled Francis a *savant*, which was a new word for the time. Francis possessed an unusual gift. This wasn't the era of PET scans where doctors are able to see computer pictures of someone's brain. But they did subject Francis to a grueling series of diagnostic tests. At the end, it was determined that because of his autism, Francis was able to use far more of his creative mind than normal people like you and me could ever hope to."

"Francis hadn't been burdened with a handicap," I said, "he'd been given a rare gift."

"Nowadays we know that savants tap into areas of the mind that function sort of like supercomputers. The computers process a massive amount of data from the senses and in turn create their own unique working model of the world."

"Thus the world-class artwork."

I thought about my own childhood, how Molly and I had become aware of a boy named Francis who lived on a nearby farm. An older boy whom some of the other kids at school referred to as a freak, even if I thought of him as Boo Radley. I hated to admit it, but there had been more than one occasion when Molly, myself, and some of our friends had snuck onto the Scaramuzzi property to get a quick look at Francis, only to be frightened away by a dog or by Mr. S himself. Standing in the basement of their home all these years later, I suddenly felt very ashamed of myself.

"Caroline," I said, "if Franny possesses the ability to tap into portions of his brain you and I can't even touch, is it possible he might possess a sixth sense? A kind of ESP?"

She looked at me with wide, unblinking dark eyes. "You mean, can Francis see the future?"

I shook my head. "Not see the future, exactly," I said. "But do you think it might be possible for him to...*sense* something that hasn't happened yet?"

She cocked her head, then shrugged. "Sure. I believe it's possible. Francis has more abilities than even I am aware of, so if he is giving you signs of something—if that's one of the reasons you have come here—it wouldn't surprise me a bit." She paused for a beat. "Is there something you're not telling me, Miss Rebecca? Something specific?"

I thought about Whalen, about his having been released from prison, his living somewhere in Albany County. I thought about all the ways of telling Caroline about him. But I knew I couldn't. Not yet. Maybe not ever. Instead, I looked at my watch.

"I should be getting back to the studio. Thank you so much for your time."

She gave me an open-eyed look before turning for the door. The look froze me. My eyes locked on her smooth face, her long gray hair, her deep eyes—eyes that read me more than looked at me. Her closed-mouth expression spoke to me better than words. It told me she knew I was hiding something. Caroline had spent the better part of a lifetime trying to communicate with a genius son who had virtually no communicative skills other than his painting. Certainly Caroline knew better than most how to read a face. I guess it would have been stupid for me to believe I could fool her.

Call it politeness or sensitivity or both, but she chose not to push me. "You're welcome here anytime," she whispered after a pause. "I miss you, your sister, your mother and father. Even though you lived a few miles away from us, it felt good to have such sweet neighbors."

There they were again: the forks of guilt stabbing at the insides of my stomach. "We weren't always great kids," I confessed.

She laughed, set a hand on my shoulder. "You mean all those times you tried to get a sneak peek at Boo Radley?"

A wash of pure humiliation poured down my back. At the same time, I thought about the ratty novel that to this day sat on my nightstand, all those sketched faces filling its margins.

"Well, allow me to let you in on something, young lady. We used to get such a kick out of scaring you kids. Francis especially enjoyed it. It was the only time you'd hear him laugh." For the first time since I arrived, I sensed her holding back a tear. "In a real way, you were his only friends."

I turned for the door. But before I stepped out, something caught my eye. A small black-and-white sketch I hadn't noticed when I walked in. The sketch was of Molly and me, back when we were about twelve years old, around the time of the assaults.

My God, Franny was drawing us back then.

"You and your sister," Caroline said. "Beautiful girls, beautiful sketch. Francis must have been about twenty-one or twenty-two when he did this."

I swallowed, because now it was me who was holding back a tear.

"Come on," Caroline said, turning off the light. "Francis is waiting for you at the School of Art."

Chapter 23

CAROLINE WAS RIGHT. FRANNY WAS WAITING FOR me. But instead of hooking a right at the end of her driveway, I turned left, drove deeper into the heart of the country. The road was narrower and more winding than I remembered it. It followed the up-and-down contours of the foothills instead of plowing right through them like in the suburbs.

After about a mile, I was able to make out Mount Desolation beyond the woods and the fields that I now called my own. The mountain was covered in the most beautiful array of autumn reds, oranges, and yellows. As it grew larger and closer, I began to feel that tingle inside of me. It was an itch that I often used to feel. The itch that signified the urge to paint. Had I brought along my easel, I might have set up outside my parents' house and reproduced that small mountain and the dark forest that surrounded it—reproduced it for the canvas, not unlike Franny had just days ago.

But I wouldn't stay there long.

Pulling up into my parents' circular driveway, the urge to create something gave way to the urge to split the scene. But that wouldn't be right. The three-story farmhouse and its wraparound porch was all that remained of my family history. As long as I was here, I had to at least make sure the place was being well cared for.

I parked the Cabriolet at the top of the drive and got out. Making my way to the front porch steps, I began to feel my heart beat. Not a frantic pounding, but a speedier than normal pulse that drummed inside my head. This house used to be a safe place for me. A place far away from the woods behind it and the man who lived in them. But now that man was free. Like me, that man might be coming home again to the woods. For all I knew, he was right behind me. But then, maybe my imagination was getting the best of me. Maybe this farm country and Mount Desolation was the last place Whalen would want to be, considering the crimes he committed there and the hard time he did for them.

I slipped the key into the lock and, twisting the knob, opened the door to that old, familiar creaking hinge. I stepped quietly inside, as though not to wake the ghosts of my family. I left the door open behind me.

The home was empty. The few pieces of furniture that remained were covered in white bedsheets that over the past ten years had turned yellow and gray. Dust and dirt, however, had been kept to a minimum thanks to the cleaning my worker gave the place once a month in exchange for the occasional painting lesson at the School of Art.

The layout of the house wasn't all that different from the Scaramuzzis', with the large combination living/dining room making up the space to my right, while behind the wall to my left was the big eat-in kitchen.

Standing alone inside the living room, I felt the bone cold that can settle into a home when the heat is turned off and no living soul occupies it. I stared at the big fieldstone fireplace my father built by hand over a period of a dozen weekends. I looked at the dark, creosote-soaked railroad-tie mantle that had once acted as a *This Is Your Life* showcase for the many framed family photos set upon it. Photos of Molly and me as babies; as toddlers learning to walk; as little girls standing squinty-eyed on a Cape Cod beach; as teenagers going off to high school, our eyes not as bright and optimistic as they should be. After all, Molly and I possessed a deep secret. And the secret ate away at us, as much as we didn't want to believe it.

Turning away from the mantle, I made my way to the center hall stairs.

I climbed.

Standing at the top of the stairs, I looked in on my parents' bedroom, their marriage bed and wedding gift bedroom furniture now long disappeared thanks to an estate sale conducted weeks after their premature deaths. It chilled me to see such an empty, lifeless space—the very place in which Molly and I had almost certainly been conceived. It chilled me to think about how it was possible for a married couple to die of grief only three months apart from one another, both of them passing away in their sleep as if it had been scripted that way.

But then, I didn't have kids. I had no idea about that kind of love, that kind of sadness. All I knew was the memory of a man who lived in those woods behind this house. And that memory had always competed with the desire to have children. Or perhaps it had killed that desire, made it impossible to contemplate.

Further down the hall was Molly's room and my room just beyond it. No longer did this upstairs vibrate to stereo systems cranked full throttle with Aerosmith and Ramones records. There was no more piped-in laugh track to the *Love Boat*, no more teary-eyed wails for *General Hospital's* super-handsome heart-throb, Scorpio.

There was nothing. And that kind of nothing was both sad and frightening.

I pictured my room with my paints and easels, the place smelling of turpentine and fresh paint, every bit of wall space covered with sketches, watercolors, and oil paintings. I pictured Molly's room, always cluttered with dirty clothes strewn about the floor, her hospital-white walls bare of even the simplest photograph, poster, or painting, as if creating a fun personal space unique to her own wants and desires was somehow undeserved or just plain useless.

While I withdrew into myself and my art after the attacks, Molly did the opposite. She would sneak out at night, meet up with some local boy, maybe go to a party or maybe just park in some isolated place at the far end of the valley. Molly never stayed with just one boy, never went steady, but strung along lots of boyfriends, while I preferred not to see anyone at all. For me, seeing a boy was an absolute impossibility considering how ugly I felt inside. I didn't even like to see myself naked.

But Molly was different. She craved the attention the boys so willingly gave her. To this day I'm amazed that she never got caught when it came time to sneak back into the house, never got nabbed red-handed by Trooper Dan. Just standing inside that hall I could once again hear the ponytailed Molly climbing up onto the porch overhang and tapping ever so gently on my window, waking me up out of a sound sleep. After climbing back through, she'd get in bed with me, and hold me, and run her hands through my hair. She'd shush me back to sleep like a mother would a baby. I'd drift away to her sweet scent and the sound of her breaths, just the two of us cocooned inside the sheets and down comforter, no different from the nine months we spent cuddled up inside our mother.

Standing inside the upstairs of that old home, I could almost feel Molly's arms wrapped around me. I could almost smell her breath. The sensations made me want to curl back up in my old bed to the memory of Molly, and never leave. But the conflict was boiling inside me. While I still felt the presence of Molly and my parents in this house, I also pictured Whalen's face, as if he were somehow staring at me from the opposite end of the hall. His memory made me want to leave this place and never come back home.

Back down on the first floor, I thought about leaving for good, maybe putting the place up for sale, getting the past out of my life forever. But then something held me back. Something had been holding me back for years now when thoughts like these visited me. Like I said, this place and the many acres of land that surrounded it were all that remained of my history. *Would selling this place erase it?*

Inhaling a deep breath, I once more made my way across the length of the living room to the large double-hung windows that made up the far window wall. I stood inches away from the glass and stared out onto the field and the dense foothill forest beyond it.

I see myself walking behind Molly as she enters the woods. I watch her disappear from view as the colorful foliage consumes her like Alice through the looking glass. I find myself standing on the edge of a sea of grass, on the edge of the known and the unknown, the accepted and the forbidden. My heart has shot up from my chest and lodged itself in my mouth while visions of my father slapping us with a punishment so severe we won't be able to leave the farm for a year.

After a few seconds (but what seems like hours), I hear Molly's voice begging for me through the trees. "Bec, come on!" she shouts. "There's a waterfall."

Curiosity pulls at my insides. It is stronger than fear. I know a man lives in these woods. A bad boogeyman. But then, maybe it's all just a story meant to scare us.

Or maybe something else is supposed to scare us away.

A waterfall.

A waterfall means a severe drop-off—a cliff of some kind. Maybe a deep pool at the bottom of it. Is that why my father has forbidden us to enter into these woods alone? The prospect of his little girls falling off of that cliff would be reason enough, right? Not the possible presence of the boogeyman.

Still, who can resist chasing a waterfall?

I take a few steps forward in the direction of Molly's voice, toward the sound of rushing water. Ducking my head, I slip through an opening in the trees, make my way into the darkness...

Chapter 24

A HOWLING WIND WOKE ME FROM MY DAYDREAM. I felt a cold draft against the right side of my face. Looking over my right shoulder, I saw that one of the double-hung windows had been left open. Not wide open, but open enough for me to feel the breeze.

Shifting myself to the window, I reached out with both hands, closed it. That's when I noticed that the old lock had been sheared as if someone had tried to force the window open from out on the porch.

I had no choice but to investigate.

Outside on the porch I went to the window and discovered that it had, in fact, been tampered with. Jimmied. Kids, teenagers. It was the first thought that entered into my head. Locals looking to do a little partying.

But then if that had been the case, there would have been beer and liquor bottles tossed all over the living room floor, maybe even the charred remnants of a fire in the fireplace.

But the place was clean. No sign of foul play, least of all a group of teen partiers.

Had Whalen paid a visit to the place? Had he forced the window open?

I had to believe that he hadn't. Had to erase the thought from my mind.

I inhaled a deep breath and made a mental note to call the worker to repair the window. I turned and started for the front door to lock it back up. It was then that I spotted the photograph. A black-and-white photo with a white border that was lying on the porch floor as if it had slipped out of somebody's pocket not ten years ago, but just this morning.

I knelt and picked the picture up.

I felt the floor beneath me shift. The image was of Molly and me. We couldn't have been more than twelve years old at the time the picture was taken. In the photo we had our twin faces up so close to the camera lens our lips were practically pressed up against it. We were playing for the camera, laughing, smiling, hamming it up for the photographer.

But this is not what robbed me of my breath and my balance. The real shock was this: the image in the photo was identical to the one I had seen inside the basement art storage space of Franny's house. The same one his mother said he'd painted back when he was still in his early twenties.

Had Franny been in possession of this photograph? How would he have gotten hold of it? Did he plant it here purposely for me to find it? If he did, how did he know that I would be coming here?

I sat down onto the porch floor, my back pressed up against the clapboard wall. I became convinced that Michael had been right all along. It wasn't just Whalen who had me spooked.

Franny was also doing a pretty good job of it.

Autism or no autism, purposely or inadvertently, Franny was playing with my head, my emotions. Somehow, I got the distinct feeling he knew all about Molly's and my secret. Somehow he'd managed to invade my head, grab hold of my memories. Now he was toying with me, dangling me by strings like a puppet.

Sweet old brilliant Franny.

I stood up, shoved the photo in my pocket, and took a three-hundred-sixty-degree look around. My fear replaced itself with anger. *Was I being followed? Stalked? Did Franny have something to do with it?*

I needed answers and I needed them now.

First I locked the door. Then made my way down the porch steps and jogged across the lawn to the Cabriolet. But before opening the door and slipping behind the wheel, I took one last look at the field and the thick woods that covered Mount Desolation.

"Up yours!"

Chapter 25

THE STUDIO WAS SILENT WHEN I ARRIVED. IF ANYONE aside from Franny and Robyn had been there while I spoke with Caroline Scaramuzzi, they were gone now. Setting my knapsack on the coat hook and my jean jacket over that, I felt the deadweight of two sets of eyes upon me. Breathing deeply, I made my way across the paint-stained floor toward Franny's corner with the same enthusiasm a condemned prisoner might face the electric chair.

"Let's see it, Fran," I said in the place of a hello.

"Bec," Robyn said, her face a painted mask of awe and wonder. "I don't know how—"

"Don't," I broke in. "Don't try and explain it."

As I came around to face the canvas, Robyn stepped off to the side, as if the corner wasn't big enough for the three of us.

"Don't, don't," Franny mumbled to himself.

"It's OK, Franny," I said. "I think I know what's happening now."

Before entering the art center just minutes before, I'd wanted to scream at Franny. *What kind of game are you playing? Why are you playing it?* I'd wanted to know if he was the one who walked to my parents' house, dropped the photograph to the porch floor. I'd wanted to know if he was the one who tried to break into the house. But looking at the newest painting (the third in three days),

I felt myself breaking down. I felt my limbs tremble, my throat close up on itself. I felt my heart lodge itself inside my sternum.

A tear rolled down my cheek.

"How is it possible for you to know these things, Fran?"

Painted on the canvas, an oil portrait of two blonde-haired girls, down on their knees at the edge of a stream. They were surrounded by deep woods. To their left was the even deeper forest. To their right, a waterfall bound on both sides by an open cliff face. Beyond that, an open valley that led further into the country. You saw only the backs of the girls, their long blonde hair draped down their narrow backs like silk veils. The girl to the left—Molly—had her hand dipped in the rushing stream water as though about to take a drink. The girl to the right—me—was looking down at the hand, curious, but at the same time, afraid to drink. At least, that's the way it had happened in real life.

That's the way I remembered it.

I stood back, pressed my spine up against the wall, my eyes glued to the painting. I took a more focused look at the woods, the girls, and the stream. Inside the water I made out the faintest of words: "taste."

I shifted my eyes to Robyn.

She appeared even more shocked now that she could see that I was crying, her normally happy-go-lucky, tanned face gone pale, her expression tight-lipped and bug-eyed. "Is that you and Molly back when you were kids?" she softly posed.

I nodded, swallowed.

She raised her right hand, pointed to the stream in the painting. "T-A-S-T-E," she spelled out. "I see the word this time, Bec. I see the word."

"Do you have a date tonight?" I whispered to her.

"Yes," she said, her eyes still focused on the painting.

"There're no more classes today," I said, wiping the tears from my face with the backs of my hands, composing myself. "I'm going to close up shop for the rest of the day. Franny and I need some privacy to talk alone."

"Alone," Franny softly spoke in rhythm with his rocking. "Alone."

Robyn shot me a pensive glance. Then, without a word, she grabbed her jacket and her bag and walked silently the length of the studio toward the exit. She turned at the door and looked not at me, but into me. "Bec, what's going on here? Why is Franny making these paintings for you?"

"I can't tell you that now. But soon I'll tell you everything."

With that worried expression still masking her face, my partner turned and disappeared out the door.

Drying my eyes once more, I swallowed a breath, tried my best to regain my equilibrium and my sanity. "Franny," I said. "It's time you and I talked the truth."

Chapter 26

AS I STOOD BEFORE FRANCIS INSIDE A STUDIO FILLED with easels, unfinished paintings, clay sculptures and sketches, and not a soul around to work on them, I found myself alone not with a man but a different creature altogether. A creature who knew something about me; about my past; about Molly's past. And, a little frighteningly, he might also know something about my future. In any case, I was determined to get the whole story out of him.

A metal work table was set only a few feet away from Franny's stool. I sat down on top of it, letting my legs dangle off the side.

"I need to ask you a few questions, Fran."

He rolled his eyes. I recognized the reaction. It meant he was receiving me loud and crystal clear. "Questions," he mumbled. "Questions, answers, questions…"

I inhaled.

"Why did you paint Molly and me, Franny? Why did you paint the woods in back of my mom and dad's home? Why are you putting words in the paintings?"

His eyes, still rolling in their sockets, never stopping to focus on anything, let alone me, for more than a couple of seconds at a time. "Molly and Rebecca," he said after a long beat. "Molly and Rebecca go into the woods. Molly and Rebecca go into the woods where they don't belong."

My stomach dropped. My pulse picked up inside my chest and temples. "What do you know about Molly and me and those woods?"

Eyes rolling rapidly inside their sockets, Franny rocked back and forth on his stool. Chubby face grew redder and redder, like a red balloon about to burst. I recalled what Caroline had said about his heart. But it didn't matter. Didn't matter enough.

"Molly and Rebecca," he chanted, voice growing louder. "Molly and Rebecca go into the woods where they don't belong. Monster man is in the woods. Monster man does bad things to Molly and Rebecca."

Body trembling, my blood shot through the veins. "Franny, how do you know this?" I said, trying not to shout, but failing. "How can you possibly know?"

I was standing now, in the middle of the studio floor. I stood over him where he was seated on the stool, left hand clutching his red T-shirt. I pulled the black-and-white photograph from my jeans pocket, held it only inches from his nose, and screamed in his face. "Did you put this on my parents' porch? How did you know I was going there? How did you know?"

But that's when something stopped me. Something invisible reached out for me, pulled me back. I collapsed onto my knees. Franny had been right here at the art center studio while I made my stopover at Caroline's. Franny could not have known that I would be visiting my childhood home. That is, unless somehow he was able to intuit it.

What have I done?

I looked up at Franny, looked at him rocking. I stood up and tried to wrap my arms around him, but he fought me off like I was a wasp that had suddenly settled on his shoulder. I gave him his space, saw that his eyes were no longer rolling but riveted at the ceiling.

I whispered, "Franny, were you there when it happened all those years ago? Did you see Joseph Whalen attack Molly and me?"

Chapter 27

HE WAS ROCKING HARD NOW, ROCKING SO VIOLENTLY on that stool I thought he might fly off. He mumbled something impossible to understand. I hated to see him like this, hated myself for causing him pain. I inhaled and exhaled until I felt some calm enter back into my bloodstream.

I shoved the photo back in my pocket and fought the urge to wrap my arms around Franny, once more try to hold him, his bulk. It would only freak him out. Instead I waited until he finally stopped rocking, though he still shivered. His big eyes were fat with tears, but not a single one fell. I wanted to dry his eyes with my hands, brush back his thick hair, shush as a mother might to calm a little boy. I pictured Caroline then, thought of how heart-wrenchingly hard it must've been to raise a child who wouldn't, couldn't bear comforting.

I told him I was sorry, that everything was going to be OK.

"OK," he whispered in a quaking voice. "Franny's OK."

When finally he calmed down, I stepped outside the room, called Caroline to come pick him up. Franny needed to go home. She was about to hang up when I stopped her. "The painting Franny brought for me today. Did you see it?"

Dead air oozed over the line.

"Francis didn't show me the piece. Sometimes he makes a point of showing the paintings to me. Other times he can be very secretive. He's a grown man and I must respect his decisions, within reason, of course."

It struck me as strange: Caroline referring to Franny as a "man." Not the boy she spoke of earlier.

We hung up.

When I went back into the studio, Franny was bundled in his old navy-blue peacoat, sticker-covered portfolio bag slung over the shoulder. He faced the door at the opposite end of the room the same way a scolded child would stand in a corner. He was awaiting his mother, even though it would be some fifteen minutes before her arrival.

The new painting was laid out on my table. Like rubbernecking at a bad car wreck, it hurt to look at it. Still, I had to pose the one crucial question about its title. But before I could open my mouth, he blurted out the answer to the unasked question.

"*Taste*," he said, not to me, but to the door only inches from his face.

Chapter 28

I RACED HOME AS SOON AS FRANNY AND HIS MOTHER took off in their old truck. Michael immediately stopped what he was doing when I came through the apartment's front door. He looked up at me, closed the laptop, as if my timing had been perfect.

"Don't tell me," he smiled warmly. "Franny painting number three."

"Sure."

He got up and stared at the painting. After a silent time, he turned to me. "You and Moll," he said. "You and Moll at the stream on the day it all happened."

I nodded.

Like Robyn before him, he traced the letters to the word "taste," which had been painted in blue-white letters inside the stream water. "I really see the word this time."

Then I told him everything else. About my morning get-together with Caroline; about the basement art room; about the painting Franny did of Molly and me many years ago—the one that precisely matched a black-and-white snapshot I just happened to discover on the porch floor of my parents' home, as if somebody had purposely set it there for me. Somebody able to anticipate my every move.

"This photo," I told him, pulling the tattered snapshot from out of my jeans pocket, setting it before him.

I told him about the jimmied window, how someone had definitely tried to break into the house. I told him about my confrontation with Franny, about how I hadn't gotten a word out of him, yet still confirmed my suspicions. That, number one, he'd somehow witnessed Whalen assaulting Molly and me thirty years ago. Maybe witnessed it through a basement window. And number two: he was trying to warn me of something. I also told him that it was time I went to the police.

Michael squinted at me. "So long as they believe you," he said, handing the snapshot back to me. "It's the right thing to do. But they've got to believe you."

My portfolio bag was stored in the narrow space between the couch and the far wall. I pulled it out, unzipped it, and took out two of my own blank canvases, setting them against the bookshelf. Then I slipped Franny's paintings inside. I zipped up the bag, slung it over my shoulder, and checked my pockets for my cell phone and car keys.

"I really want you to come with me," I said. "But if you'd rather keep out of it…"

He pursed his lips and shot me a wink of his right eye. "Let's go make believers out of the cops," he said.

Chapter 29

OUR DECISION TO DRIVE DOWNTOWN TO THE SOUTH Pearl Street Precinct had not been indiscriminate. According to the info we'd found online, this was the very place in which Whalen had been jailed after his arrest for the abduction and attempted rape of an eighteen-year-old college freshman thirty years ago. That single assault led to the discovery of at least a half dozen prior rapes when, after a photo of Whalen was posted on every local TV station and newspaper, a small flood of brave, young women started coming forward and pointing the finger—women with more courage than Molly and me. Or maybe less to lose by telling the truth.

Being that my father had been a state trooper, I wasn't entirely a stranger to police stations. But that didn't make them any more comfortable to be around. I slung my cumbersome portfolio bag over my shoulder, and followed Michael up the granite steps across the vestibule to the large bench where a heavyset, gray-haired officer sat. Before his desktop computer and phone, a small plaque bore the embossed words, "Watch Commander."

"Help you?" he grumbled, eyes focused not on us but his computer screen.

"We need to speak with a detective," Michael announced.

Behind the watch commander's shoulder, I could make out the not-too-unfamiliar inner workings of the wide-open station—the many uniformed and plainclothes policemen and women, the identical metal desks set out equidistant from one another, each of them topped with a computer where typewriters might have been back when Whalen was first arrested. Back when my dad was Trooper Dan. There were the bright overhead lights, the ringing phones, the chiming cells, the buzzing fax machines and at least a dozen voices competing with one another.

"And why is it you need to see a detective?" the watch commander asked his screen.

I took a step forward. "I have reason to believe I'm being stalked by a sexual predator."

The old cop at last pulled his eyes away from the computer. "Come again," he said, looking into my face.

"I'm being followed."

Behind his shoulder, I saw that two people were taking notice. Police detectives, or so I suspected. An older man and a middle-aged woman, both dressed in normal, everyday plainclothes.

"Do you have an ID of this supposed stalker?" asked the watch commander.

I hesitated, as though the question had shot over my head. I didn't want to say the man's name, as if doing so would make me physically sick.

"He's asking if you know for certain that it's Whalen who is stalking you?" Michael jumped in.

I nodded. "Yeah, I can identify the man."

"You mentioned a name," the watch commander added, eyes now on Michael.

"Joseph William Whalen," Michael said. "He's registered with Sexual Predators and with ViCAP."

"Oh, ViCAP, huh?" The old cop smiled. "Looks like you been doin' your homework."

"I write detective novels," Michael said.

"Of course you do. Wait here a minute please."

He got up, made his way over to the two plainclothes cops. He talked with them while they looked us over again. When the older, male cop approached, I felt my pulse pick up.

"My name is David Harris," the tall, salt-and-pepper-haired black man said. "I understand you're here to lodge a complaint?"

"I have reason to believe I'm being followed."

"By Joseph Whalen?"

"Yes."

"You'd better come on through," he said. "I know Whalen. I know about what he's done and what he might have done to more than a dozen still-missing young women."

A wave of ice water washed over me. Molly had been right all along. Whalen hadn't just sexually abused girls and women. He was a killer. He would've killed us, but we got away—thanks to Molly.

"Just how well do you know him, Detective?"

"Considering I'm the one who busted him thirty years ago, I'd say very well."

Chapter 30

THE WATCH COMMANDER BUZZED US IN. BUT NOT before making us sign the logbook and issuing us laminated visitor's passes, which we clipped onto our jackets.

Harris led us through the big open room to his first-floor office, where he closed the door behind us and offered us a seat as he made his way around his desk to his swivel chair.

I sat down in one of the two metal chairs placed in front of the desk, while Michael thanked Harris, but revealed he'd prefer to remain standing since he spends all day sitting in front of his laptop. Leaning the bag against my knees, I took a quick survey of the office. It was square and small. It smelled faintly of onions, as if Harris had just lunched on a submarine sandwich at his desk. There was a coffee mug on his desk that said "I love my job." When he picked it up and took a sip from it, I could see the word "Not" printed on the bottom. It made me smile.

Mounted on the windowless wall behind him was a calendar. Each day that had passed thus far in the month of October had been X'd out in ballpoint pen. In just a little while he'd be able to X out another day.

Harris must have noticed me looking at the calendar. He said, "I'm closing in on retirement. The progressive-minded Empire State doesn't have much use for its detectives once we get past sixty-two."

He shrugged, rolled up his shirtsleeves, and sat back in his chair. "But to get back to the issue at hand," he went on. "As it happens, I was a part of the team that tracked Whalen down and eventually arrested him. That was back in '77 and '78. We'd been tracking him for a long while. We were aware of his past, the horrors inflicted upon him as a child and the horrors he inflicted upon his family in retaliation. We're also aware of his past as a sexual predator and suspected him in at least a dozen abductions and possible homicides. But we could never quite put the finger on him."

"Impossible for the dead and missing to testify," Michael interjected. "No body, no proof."

Harris nodded. "Exactly. It goes back to the bodies, none of which have been recovered. Which means no evidence that will link directly to Whalen."

"You might check the basement of that creepy house in the woods."

"We did, on several occasions." The detective tossed up his hands. "But aside from some unidentifiable bone fragments, we got squat."

We were quiet for a weighted beat while I tried to comprehend the evil that resided in Whalen's body, and in that house in the woods. Whenever I pictured him, I couldn't help but hear the screams of his victims. Young women. Girls. Molly. Myself. I pictured us running in the woods, trying to get away from him. Saw it all happening again, until Michael spoke up once more. "Are you aware that Whalen's been released from prison?"

Almost dreamily, Harris peeled his eyes off the mug, planted them on Michael. "I'm aware of it," he said, nodding. "I try and keep up on the perps I had a hand in sending away. It's in my best interest to keep up with their releases."

"Watching for reoffenders, or watching your back?" Michael asked.

"Sometimes both. But not so much in this case, either way. Whalen's exactly my age. But he's an old sixty-two, since he's spent most of that time behind bars in an iron house that's not very well known for its hospitality. He's also been quiet. He's registered with the necessary databases according to Megan's Law. He checks in regularly with his parole officer."

"You're sure about that?" I asked.

His eyes shifting back to me. "I would be aware of it if he didn't."

"But you wouldn't be aware of it if he was following me."

"I'm aware of that possibility now," he said. "But I'm going to need a little more to go on than just your word before I can go pulling him back in here. The last thing I need is a harassment accusation."

That's when I unzipped my portfolio bag and slipped out Franny's paintings.

Harris eyed the canvases quickly up and down. Then he looked at me rather quizzically. "You're an artist?"

"I wish I could say I painted them. But they're the work of an artist-in-residence where I work at the Albany Art Center. His name is Francis Scaramuzzi. He's an autistic savant. You might have heard of him."

He shook his head, sat back in his chair. "What's all this have to do with Whalen?"

I swallowed a deep breath and told him. I told him about the abduction and assault that occurred thirty years ago, almost to the day. I told him about Franny's paintings, told him about the voice I heard in my bedroom, told him about the man I might have seen inside the parking garage.

I thought the wall plaster would crack from the silent tension. Finally Harris brought his hands to his face, rubbed his eyes. "Well, I can see why you'd be rattled and looking over your shoulder every two minutes. Whalen's taken up way more space in you and your sister's lives than he has any right to. He's a major creep, and he's done awful things to lots of women, you two included. And now he's out."

"But?"

A tired smile. "Right. But."

"But these paintings and my creepy feelings don't exactly add up to much, in terms of bringing Whalen back in."

Harris gave an apologetic shrug, nodding. "Couldn't have put it better myself." Another rueful smile. "You sound like you have some experience in law enforcement."

"My dad was a trooper with Rensselaer County."

Harris pursed his lips. "That right? What's his name?"

"It *was* Daniel Underhill. He and my mother passed away not long after my sister died."

He gave no indication of whether he knew my father or not; no indication of whether or not my father might have had a hand in Whalen's arrest. I guess I'd always kind of hoped he had.

Instead he said, "Tell you what, Ms. Underhill, I'm going to request that you leave the paintings with me for a while. I'll have the lab draw up a print analysis. That is, if you don't mind."

"They're kind of expensive," Michael said.

"Don't worry, Mr. Hoffman. The lab people are very careful. They'll be well cared for." Eyes back on me. "Have you considered seeing your psychologist about this, Ms. Underhill? Or is it Hoffman?"

"Please, call me Rebecca," I said. "And I'm not crazy, if that's what you're thinking."

He shook his head, raised his hands in surrender. "I'm sure you're not. But keeping a secret of the magnitude you have for all these years can be traumatizing. A psychologist can treat you for PTS."

"You think my wife's been experiencing post-traumatic stress, Detective Harris?" Michael interjected.

The cop cocked his head. "It's possible," he said.

"Gentlemen," I said. "I'm not crazy."

Harris got up.

I stood up along with him.

"I'll tell you what I'm willing to do," he said. "I'm going to give Whalen's probie a call before I leave tonight, find out where he's living, what he's doing for a job. If he lives and works anywhere near you, I'm going to alert New York State Sexual Predators about it. With your permission, of course."

I nodded.

"Is there anything else you want to tell me before you go? Anything else you need to show me?"

I thought about it as I slung the bag over my shoulder. That's when I recalled the old black-and-white photo. Reaching into my jeans pocket, I set the snapshot onto his desk.

"What's this?" he said, picking it up with his fingers by the narrow white border.

I told him.

"So you found this picture only this morning on the porch of your parents' Brunswick home?"

"It perfectly matches a little painting Francis Scaramuzzi produced years ago. A painting that is now stored under lock and key inside his personal basement storage room."

He shook his head, rolled his eyes. "Strange coincidence, I will admit," he said. "I'd like to hold onto this as well, check it for prints along with the paintings."

"You have my blessing."

"You sure that's everything?" he asked once more.

I spotted Harris's cell phone on the desktop, which made me think of the strange texts I'd been receiving. I went to open my mouth about it, but something held me back. I knew I should have told Harris everything. But something inside my gut stopped me from doing the right thing.

Something entirely to do with Molly.

I knew that if I told Harris about the texts, he might confiscate my cell and look for a way to break into the database to find a way to expose the unknown caller's ID. It didn't make much sense, but I feared that might take away my only physical link to Molly.

Michael slipped on his jacket and his beret. Harris took special notice of the beret, squinting his eyes as he slipped out from behind his desk. He opened the office door, held it open for us.

"I understand you write detective novels, Mr. Hoffman," he smiled. "Anything published?"

"*The Hounds of Heaven*," Michael said. "Came out a few years ago. I'm working on something new right now."

Reaching into his pocket, the detective handed us each a card. "Give me a call if anything else happens," he said. "Call anytime, day or night. My cell number is also on there."

I thanked him.

He told me not to worry; to get a good night's rest.

As we started to walk out, I said, "I do have one more question, Detective."

His eyebrows perked up.

"You never asked me why my sister and I didn't come to you about the attack thirty years ago."

He picked at his right earlobe quickly with an extended index finger. "I've been working this job for thirty-eight years," he said with a resignation I hadn't noticed until now. "I know precisely why you didn't come to me, Rebecca. It's absolutely understandable, and unfortunately, not at all uncommon."

With that I turned, led Michael toward the exit. When we handed in our visitor's passes to the watch commander, he asked us to have a nice day. But it seemed a little late for that.

Chapter 31

"WHY DIDN'T YOU TELL HIM ABOUT THE TEXTS?"

Michael was speaking to me out the side of his mouth as he pulled out of the police station onto South Pearl Street.

I turned to him, watched his profile while he drove. "Why didn't *you* tell him?"

He was quiet for a minute, pretending to concentrate on the road when in fact he was filled with thought. "It's your call," he said after a while. "I know how you feel about the texts, about them coming from..." He allowed his thought to dangle, as if it were too strange for him to say it.

"Coming from Molly," I uttered for him. "From heaven above. You don't have to be afraid to say it."

"The tangible proof you need that heaven exists? That God exists? That Molly lives? A cell phone?"

I couldn't help but smile.

"I still think you should have told the dick," he added.

"I will tell him. As soon as I can convince myself that Molly has nothing to do with it."

We let the subject drop. But our silence didn't lighten things up for even a moment. By the time we approached my apartment complex, I was so nervous, so pent up with anxiety, I felt like jumping out of my skin.

Michael took notice of my apprehension. He thought it would be a good idea for us simply to head into the apartment, lock ourselves behind closed doors, and do something we hadn't done together in ages: cook.

It felt like a good idea; a comforting idea. It's exactly what we did, even though I wasn't particularly hungry. It had been a long time since I'd shared a dinner with a man. Hell, it'd been a long time since I cooked for myself. Anything other than Stouffer's. My kitchen shelves were not exactly stocked with food.

But Michael wasn't the least bit fazed. Crossing his arms over his chest, he staunchly replied that he would make do with whatever I had. Which pretty much consisted of three boxes of wheat pasta and some tomato sauce.

"Minimalism." Michael smiled. "Simply perfect. Like a Ray Carver short story."

"A rose is a rose is a rose," I recited.

"Gertrude Stein," he stated proudly.

He filled a large pot with cold tap water then set it onto the gas stove to boil. He uncorked a bottle of red, poured us each a glass, and took them with him into the living room. While I slipped the new Belarus disk into the CD player, he sat down on the couch, exhaling a long sigh.

"Feel better?" he said, taking a small sip of wine. "I know I do. In a proactive sort of way."

I listened for the music to begin. Slowly strummed guitar, smoothly exhaled harmonica, deep bass, steady drums. Voices followed. Harmonious and rich, and like all good art, able to touch me in the spot that made tears press up against the backs of my eyeballs.

I shuffled around the coffee table, sat myself down on the couch beside my ex-husband. I picked up my wine, took a small sip.

"I'm not entirely sure what I feel."

"Harris is looking out for you now. That's gotta mean something, afford you just a semblance of peace. Even if you did avoid the issue of the texts."

"I got the distinct feeling he thought I was out of my head." Turning to Michael, I continued: "In fact, I'm starting to feel the same way. That maybe I'm just a little nutty; that maybe much of what's happened over the past few days *is* in my head." I laughed. "Heaven-sent text messages, for God's sake. I'm not even sure I believe in God anymore!"

"Oh ye of little faith, huh?" Michael said, taking a large swallow of wine.

"I don't know what to believe sometimes."

"You can't deny Franny's paintings," he pointed out. "You can't deny seeing the words in them."

"Why is it so much more difficult for other people to see the words?"

"It's just easier for you to see them. Or maybe you *want* to see them."

"OK, so what else can't I deny?"

"You mean what else proves you're not a nutcase?"

"Sure."

"You can't deny that the images Franny paints are similar to your dreams."

"No, I can't. But not even Franny is gifted enough to be inside my head." I paused. "Or is he?"

Cocking his head, Michael exhaled. "Maybe he's in tune with you. Your thoughts and fears. I think that he does somehow see your dreams, and paint them. He has no choice but to paint them for you. He *wants* you to see your dreams through your conscious eyes."

I believed what Michael was telling me, but could just as easily look at it all as a remarkable coincidence. *How could I deny the painting of me and Molly stored inside Franny's basement? How could I deny the identical black-and-white snapshot I found on my parents' porch? How could I deny Whalen's release from prison?*

Maybe I wasn't nuts after all. Maybe everything was somehow fitting into place. Maybe Whalen truly was a threat. Maybe Franny knew this and was doing everything in his power to warn me.

I rested my head back against the couch. "I'm thinking about taking the next couple of days off," I said. "Stay close to home until this thing blows over and Harris can ensure my safety."

"Good idea," Michael agreed. "You can sleep in while I bite the nail." He smiled. "Like we used to do in the old days."

I thought about the old days. Back when *The Hounds of Heaven* was first published. Michael and I spent a lot of time in New York City back then. We'd stay at the Gramercy Park Hotel on Lexington Avenue. In the mornings Michael would run the paved path that ran parallel to the East River. I'd sleep in until he came back, body damp from the jog, a paper bag in one hand filled with hot croissants, a second bag in the other holding two large coffees with milk. He'd tiptoe around the room while he undressed and showered, and if I was still sleeping he'd write at the hotel desk, dressed in nothing but his bath towel, until I woke up. That's when he'd slip back into bed with me and we'd have our breakfast and plan out our day while we ate fresh croissants with jam and drank coffee, our bare feet touching under the covers. Back then it had never been the things that Michael said to me that made me feel secure with him. It was the things he did for me.

Without thinking about it, I slipped my hand in his. He turned to me, set his wine glass gently onto the coffee table, moved into me, and started kissing me.

I kissed him back but then pulled away. "We should eat." I smiled.

From where we were sitting I could hear the water boiling on the stove in the kitchen.

"Do you want me to spend the night?" Michael softly spoke.

I turned to him, looked into his brown eyes. I could see his desire to protect me. "If you're going to stay, I suggest you call your mother first."

"She doesn't wait up anymore. I'm forty-three years old, don't forget."

I shook my head, rolled my eyes. Maybe this was a bad idea. Or maybe not. But just the mere suggestion of Michael staying with me proved a comfort.

"I'll go put in the pasta," he said. "You relax."

He got up, went into the kitchen. As much as I wanted to take his advice and just relax, I knew I should be giving Robyn a call. It was important that I tell her about my plan to take the next couple of days off. After all, the School of Art studio classes had to go on, not to mention the midmonth meeting with the board of directors.

I got up from the couch and located my phone in my jean jacket pocket. I speed-dialed Robyn and surprisingly got her message service; she always picked up my calls. I left a message anyway, telling her about the days I would be taking off. Before I hung up,

I decided to tell her that I would be having some company tonight in the form of my ex-husband.

"Please don't call past nine," I said.

Unlike Robyn, I didn't get a thrill out of answering the phone while snuggling up with a date.

Chapter 32

AFTER DINNER I ASKED MICHAEL TO CHECK THE DOORS and windows in the apartment. By the time he came back in, I was already in bed, waiting for him. *Was I making the right decision by letting him stay over? Was I being an idiot? Was all this happening way too fast?*

Somehow my sudden desire to be close to him overrode common sense. With only a lit candle set out on the dresser to see by, he slipped in under the comforter and gave me a warm smile.

It'd been a long time since I shared a bed with my ex-husband. You might think I'd be all over him, and he all over me. But inside that dimly lit room, with only the flickering candlelight glowing against the plaster walls, we lay on our sides facing one another, looking into each other's eyes, not saying a single word but shouting out volumes.

For more than a few instances, it seemed almost as if we'd never been separated or divorced, never spent even one minute away from one another. I wondered how it could be that two people who loved each other could not find a way to live together. But then I also had to wonder what still attracted us to each other after all we'd been through. And now, too, after the secret I had revealed to him.

After a time, Michael reached out and touched my face. The gentle gesture sent a chill through my body. He leaned into me, kissing me on the mouth. I kissed him back. He moved in closer, then slid one arm under me and the other around me. He pulled me close to him and he held me. He held me so tightly, I thought he'd never let go. And when he began to cry, so did I. I felt our tears combining and I tasted the salt from them, and we hardly made a sound other than the beating of our hearts.

For that brief eternity I was him and he was me and there was no past or future. There was only the sweet right now and all the wrongs that had occurred between us—all the hurt and all the pain—had suddenly and very definitely disappeared. In a word, Michael and I were new again. The love that had died had been resurrected.

If there indeed was a God, He truly did work in mysterious ways. Maybe He'd taken away the sister I adored more than myself, but somehow, He'd given me back Michael. He'd given me back my soul mate.

After a time, we lay on our backs feeling content and happy, holding hands, staring at the ceiling, not speaking or needing to speak, but just watching the flame-shadows that danced upon every surface that surrounded us from floor to ceiling. Set beside me on the table, my old dog-eared copy of *To Kill a Mockingbird*, its now-delicate pages stuffed with sketches of Whalen from thirty years ago. As I lay in bed, I felt like taking one of the candles to it and lighting it on fire. I felt like destroying it and my past. But I knew I wouldn't.

Michael got out of bed, replaced the comforter over me, then blew out the candle and slipped back in bed. He took hold of a small tuft of my hair. He let it rest in his fingertips, allowing his hand to sit on my pillow.

"Love you, Bec," he whispered. "Don't be afraid."

Maybe four minutes later I was listening to the sound of his breathing as he slept soundly. For that one moment I felt happier than I'd felt in years.

I fell asleep to that happiness.

Chapter 33

I'M WALKING WITH MOLLY ALONG A STREAM BANK
surrounded by trees. The water flows as wide and heavy as a river.
In the dream I'm walking right beside her, but I am also seeing the
entirety of the dream as though looking at a movie screen.

Although no one is speaking I know we are looking for a place
to cross the wide stream in order to go deeper into the forest. This is
a forbidden place, but I am too far gone now, too far into the woods
to go back. My only choice is to follow Moll, keep my eyes peeled on
her red Paul McCartney and Wings T-shirt.

Soon we come upon a place in the stream that is shallower than
the rest. There's a series of boulders that rise out of the moving water.
The boulders form a natural land bridge.

Molly turns to me, that smile on her face wider than ever. "Here,"
she exclaims, as though she's been looking for the spot all along.
It's then that I know for certain Molly has been here before. She's
defied our father, explored the woods without his OK, and without
my knowledge.

"Stay close," she orders as we traverse the rock bridge to the other
side of the stream. "There, I can almost see it."

Molly knows something is out there. It's why she made me go
into the woods with her in the first place.

We walk maybe another one hundred yards before that thing takes shape.

"You see it, Bec?" Molly shouts. "Can you see it?"

I can see it by then. As amazing as it seems, as buried as it is in the trees, I see it as clearly as I see Molly before me.

A house set in the middle of the woods.

Then a noise.

My cell phone vibrating.

And a voice.

"Rebecca."

Chapter 34

THE NAME WAS NEITHER SCREAMED NOR SPOKEN. IT came to me as a kind of whisper. Or maybe it just came to me. Maybe it just happened inside my head.

The cell phone vibrated.

I thought I heard movement coming from inside the living room. I sensed movement, anyway, the same way an expecting mother might sense her baby's first kick. Heavy, booted feet shuffling against the hardwood.

My prone body was bolted to the bed. It wasn't a bed at all, but a rigid platform and I was bolted and chained to it.

My heart drummed triplets against my ribcage.

Had my cell phone really been ringing? Was this a repeat of two nights ago? Had I heard a voice? A whisper? Had it all been a dream?

"Rebecca."

Again. The voice had personality. It was gruff and low. There were specific details to the voice. There was a smell that went with that voice.

The smell of stale cigarettes. I knew that smell. Cigarette butts.

Eyes wide open, unblinking, I swear I saw a shadow. The shadow of a man staring back at me from the open bedroom door, as if someone were standing inside the open frame—a silhouette against the darkness.

Was Whalen standing there, looking back at me? Had he violated his parole by sneaking out of the halfway house to come here?

I swear it's him.

Footsteps along the floor outside the bedroom door. The filthy ashtray smell. The cell phone vibrating and chiming.

If only I could lift my arms. If only I could reach out and grab hold of the phone. If only.

I wanted to scream. But want and desire were meaningless.

I felt the presence of Michael beside me. We were not divorced. We were still married and he was sleeping soundly right next to me, close to me, his body curled into my side, his face facing me. Just like it's always been.

His sleeping breaths were not the least bit bothered by the sounds, the smells, the sights taking place inside this bedroom in the middle of the deep night.

"Rebecca."

Every nerve in my body tingled.

I can't possibly be dreaming. Can't possibly be dreaming. Can't possibly be dreaming...

I made a wish. Wished the voice away; wished the smell away; wished the figure of a small, thin man away.

The man who took Molly and me.

I began to drift.

As though by some miracle, I started falling.

Faster.

Then faster still...

Chapter 35

WHEN I WOKE UP, THE SUN WAS SHINING THROUGH the windows. It seemed like a beautiful day, the terrible dream sounds, smells, and sights of the night far behind me. But not far enough. I picked up my cell and peeked at the time.

Six thirty.

My hands trembling, I opened the phone to see if someone had called me during the night.

Nothing. Not even a new text.

I had dreamt the text. But had I dreamt Whalen's presence in my apartment?

I could only hope that I had.

Michael was still asleep. I decided to leave him be. Or maybe I just wanted some time to myself. Time to breathe, get my act together. I needed my routine. Craved it.

I got up, threw on a robe to fight off the chill, and got to work on making the coffee. I swallowed a vitamin with a tall glass of orange juice, tried to eat my two ounces of Frosted Mini Wheats, but only managed a couple of bites.

As the rich aroma of the coffee filled the apartment, I checked the living room. I walked from one end to the other, examining the floor, the couch, the desk, the bookshelves.

Nothing seemed out of order; nothing seemed as if it had been tampered with. No footprints on the floor, no handprints on the walls. I looked over the windows and the door that led out onto the stone terrace for fingerprints or smudges on the panes and sills.

Nothing. All deadbolts and safety chains secured.

What about the bathroom?

I crossed over the vestibule, traversed the narrow hall that accessed my bedrooms and rarely used painting studio, and entered the bathroom. I checked the window over the toilet.

The window was bigger than it needed to be. A man could climb in through it. But it was closed.

Reaching up and under the shade, I felt for the lock. It was unlatched. A jolt of electricity shot through my veins. *Was it possible that my apartment had been broken into? Had Whalen opened this window from the outside, climbed in through it, slipped into my apartment and my bedroom, whispered into my ear?* Just because no visible evidence of a break-in existed didn't mean that it hadn't happened. I remembered him as a small man. Maybe even small and still agile enough to fit through that open window.

I couldn't help thinking that Whalen had made his physical presence known inside my apartment last night. Or was I just plain crazy, like Harris had suggested? The victim of the dreaded PTS? The victim of vivid nightmares?

I locked the bathroom window. Then I went into the kitchen, poured a cup of coffee, sipped it carefully. I tightened my robe against the chill. The old radiant heat system was blasting, but I was shivering cold.

What was happening to me? Harris wasn't kidding when he suggested I see a psychiatrist. Post-traumatic stress. Today I would fess up to the detective about the texts. Michael was right. I should never have kept the truth from the cop for even a single day.

I took another sip of the coffee. It tasted bittersweet. Today was Thursday. Would Franny have a new painting for me today? Would he be upset that I wasn't around to see it? That I was spoiling his routine?

Smell and *Touch.*

Those were the only senses left. They would be the titles of the final two paintings.

I drank some more coffee, picked up my cell phone, and punched the instant dial-up for Robyn. Again, the answering service popped on.

Why in God's name wasn't she picking up?

Noise came from the bedroom. Michael was up.

Should I tell him about sensing Whalen in our bedroom last night while we slept? Tell him about hearing his voice, smelling his stale-cigarette smell? About the open bathroom window? My sense of reason said, yes, tell him everything. But caution told me to shut up about it. Shut up for now. Last night had been as perfect a night as I'd had in years. The last thing I wanted was to spoil it all this morning—spoil it for us. Michael was back in tune with me, with my thoughts and fears. He was here to protect me. I wanted to give him some peace, some space from whatever was happening to me. Was a little peace too much to ask?

"Rebecca?" he called out from the bedroom. "What time is it?"

I grabbed a second mug from the cabinet.

Michael would need a good jolt of coffee before he started biting the nail.

Chapter 36

AN HOUR LATER, I WAS GETTING OUT OF THE SHOWER when the buzzer sounded on the front door. Michael was at his writing desk in the living room. I heard him curse as he got up from the table and tended to the interruption.

While I towel-dried my hair before the mirror, I heard him open the apartment door, then head up the small set of concrete stairs to the building's main entrance and open that door.

No words exchanged. At least, from where I stood in the bathroom, I didn't hear any.

After a few seconds, Michael came back into the apartment, closing the door behind him.

I stepped out of the bedroom.

With one towel wrapped around my body, another wrapped around my hair, I saw him standing in the small vestibule, a thin, square package in his hands. The package looked a whole lot like a canvas wrapped in brown butcher's paper.

Standing beside Michael, I began to feel the now too familiar blood-pressure increase; the usual dry mouth; the queasiness in my stomach.

Michael just stared at me, the package gripped in his hands. Neither one of us had to say a word to know what it was.

"Open it," I said.

"How about I just chuck it out?"

"Open it. We can't just ignore it."

He exhaled, stuck a finger through the paper, tore into it, and pulled it away from the painting. Immediately, even before all the paper was torn away, I recognized the scene. It was a house in the woods. *The* house in the woods. The one from my dream; the one from my past. Whalen's house. The house my sister found some weeks before me while on one of her secret expeditions into the forbidden woods. The house I remembered so well; a house that appeared not to have been built from wood, brick, and stone, but to have grown up in the forest out of nothing at all; a house that to me had sprung up from the ground like a thorn bush but that to Molly had seemed like a miracle.

The painting was a realistic rendering of that old, long-forgotten farmhouse. The house was set in the middle of a second growth forest that had grown up all around it, consumed it for its own once its original owners had died off or simply abandoned it.

Pulling the rest of the brown paper from the piece, Michael stared down at the image. My eyes began to tear. I took a tentative step forward toward my distant past, stood not beside my ex-husband but up against him. My unfocused eyes viewed Franny's painting, but I did not see a static rendering of brown tress or overgrown pines or the heavy brush or the gray-brown clapboard house that stood in its center. My eyes instead saw the real events of that day, like watching a real-time film that was somehow being broadcast on the canvas itself.

Molly leads me through the woods, bushwhacking our way through the thick growth, twigs and branches slapping at our exposed faces, at our bare arms and legs, making our eyes tear from the sting. When we come upon the old two-story farmhouse it is like a vision or an illustration out of an old storybook—Little Red Riding Hood maybe; a secret place in the forest that would be entirely familiar to the Big Bad Wolf. It is a long-abandoned farmhouse on a farm given over to nature, nature devouring any trace of humankind beyond the house's four walls and sagging roof.

The closer we come to the dilapidated and rotting clapboard house, the more I can smell a foul odor. It is an odor I sometimes recognize when walking over a sewer grate.

Molly turns to me, clothespins her nose and nostrils with the forefinger and thumb of her right hand; does it more for show than for the need to block out the rancid smell. "It's the old septic system, Bec," she explains while stepping onto a front porch that has all but collapsed into the earth from rot and neglect.

"God, how did you find this place, Mol?" I ask her, careful to breathe through my mouth instead of my nose. But what I really want to ask her is if the boogeyman lives here. I'm just too afraid to ask her.

"It's always been here." She smiles. "The house just kind of found me." Holding up her hands as if to say Voila! "It's our place now; our secret fairytale castle in the forest; our hideaway home away from home."

I find myself just staring at my sister who is me in every way, but so different at the same time. I'm not sure what I'm more amazed at: her or the discovery of this house and the possibility of having it all to ourselves. Unlike Molly, I'm half scared out of my wits. There's a reason our father does not want us in these woods. At first I blamed the stream, the waterfall, and the sudden drop-off in the hillside. But now I blame this old decaying house set in the middle of nowhere. It's a scary place. A place a boogeyman would live. I want to turn around. Go home. But this is Molly's party now. You don't say no to Molly.

Molly goes up to the front door and tosses me another one of her irresistible John Wayne "Move 'em out" waves. She sets a hand on the old, blackened knob and, lowering her shoulder like a running back about to take on some linebackers, shoves the door open...

"Rebecca," Michael barked. "What is this place?"

But I couldn't answer him yet, couldn't find the words inside my brain or my heart. I didn't have it in me to speak. Instead I looked at the trees and the house and I saw it all in my mind like it was only yesterday: our entry through the front door into the dark home, the spider-webbed interior, the horrible stench that I tasted more on my tongue than smelled through my nose.

I touched the home with my fingertips, running the pad of my left index finger along the five red-brown letters that made up the word "smell," the letters tattooed along the side of the house like graffiti.

"Smell," Michael read, the word pouring like acid off his lips.

He could see the word clearly. It told me that Franny no longer felt the need to hide his titles. Franny was screaming at me now. On Monday, when no one but me could recognize the word in his painting, he'd been whispering. Now that everyone could see the word, he was screaming—screaming for me to use my senses, to pay attention, to watch my back.

"What. Is. This. Place?" Michael repeated.

I swallowed. He knew all about my secret. He knew exactly what this place was. He just needed to hear it from me, from my mouth. "It's the house in the woods," I said. "It's where Whalen took Molly and me."

Confirming his worst fear, Michael cocked the painting over his head and threw it across the room.

Chapter 37

IT WAS UP TO ME TO CALM MICHAEL DOWN. IT DIDN'T matter now how I tried to preserve the happiness of the previous night; Franny's painting, his warning, had ruined the moment.

My ex-husband was sitting on the edge of the couch, hands pressed against his face, muttering something about "tearing Franny a new one."

"It's not his fault," I protested. "Franny is simply doing what Franny does. I know without a doubt now that he's *talking* to me, Michael, not trying to torment me."

Michael lifted his head. He was sporting a three-day shadow to go with his mustache and goatee. "Then why does it *feel* like torment?"

I picked the painting up off the floor and slipped it inside my art bag, out of sight, out of spinning mind. I fully intended to personally deliver it to Harris, just like I fully intended to reveal the texts.

Michael wiped both eyes with the backs of his hands. "What's going on here, Bec?" he insisted. "Why would Franny drop the painting off to the apartment instead of leaving it at the art center? That was the whole point behind your taking a couple of days off."

"I don't know," I sighed. "But I'm about to find out."

Drawing in a deep breath, I pulled my towel tighter over my chest and walked barefoot into the bedroom to get dressed. After that, I was going to call Robyn and find out why she gave Caroline and Franny permission to make a surprise drive-by to my home.

Chapter 38

MICHAEL STOOD BY MY SIDE WHILE I SPEED-DIALED Robyn's number and waited for a pickup. For the third time in a row, I was greeted by her answering service.

My pulse picked up. This was so *not* like Robyn.

The fact that Franny and his mother made the effort to deliver the fourth painting directly to my door told me that Robyn had not showed up to open the art center that morning. Otherwise Franny would have simply left the fourth painting there for me.

I dialed the number for the center. I waited for a pickup, but got the answering machine and my own digitally recorded voice: *"You've reached the Albany Art Center. No one is available…"*

My call waiting kicked in. Pulling the phone away from my ear, I looked at the number displayed on the readout. The number did not catch my attention. But the caller ID did.

Albany Medical Center.

With trembling fingers, I clicked over to receive the call.

A woman spoke to me in a hesitant whisper, almost like she was being held hostage. Sobs punctuated her whispers.

Robyn's mother, June.

"Rebecca," she cried, "I…have…some…"

She let the sentence hang, as though to complete it was simply too painful.

Michael was staring at me. His shadowy face had gone pale. He opened his mouth as if to say something, but I raised my open hand and pulled my eyes away from his, stopping him cold.

"June," I begged. "What's happened?" I tried to keep my voice steady, even. I'd known Robyn's mother almost as long as I'd known Robyn. I'd never heard her so upset.

"Albany Medical Center," she exclaimed. "ICU. Please come."

I dry-swallowed. "Is she alive, June? Is…Robyn…alive?"

"She's alive," June whispered.

Then she hung up.

Wide-eyed, Michael gazed expectantly into my face.

"Something bad has happened to Robyn," I explained. "I have to go."

"You get your stuff together," Michael said. "I'll wait for you out in the truck."

He took me by surprise. There had been a time in our lives when no emergency, big or small, would have kept him from his daily word quota. As he gathered his jacket and beret and headed out the front door to his pickup, I had to ask myself, *Who is this man?*

Acting on instinct, I grabbed my art bag and exited the apartment by way of the back door.

Chapter 39

THE ALBANY MEDICAL CENTER ICU WAS BRIGHTLY LIT. It was filled with doctors and nurses competing for floor space with the portable gurneys, monitors, hand carts, wheeled IV units, desks, counters, and chairs.

The nurse at the counter pointed us in Robyn's direction. Like all the beds in the unit, hers was hidden behind a sea-blue curtain. From beneath the curtain, I could make out June's sneaker-covered feet and the tattered cuffs on her gray slacks. The feet were planted stone still on the vinyl tiled floor. A gauze bandage had been tossed on the floor not two or three inches from her feet. The bandage was stained with blood.

My heart was pounding so fast I was having trouble keeping my balance. Michael took hold of my arm. I reached out for the curtain, but I wasn't sure if I possessed the strength to pull it aside.

"Rebecca," Michael whispered.

"It's OK." I swallowed. I slid back the curtain.

Her face was swelled and bruised, her eyes puffed up and closed shut, her lips bruised and blistered. I didn't dare look for any missing teeth.

Robyn's beautiful face.

It came as a relief that she'd been sedated. *What in God's name would 1 say to her? What could 1 say?*

A clear plastic tube had been run up her left nostril. Her left arm and hand were positioned atop the bed beside her, palm up. An intravenous line was needled into her vein. Hooked to the hospital bed's plastic railing, a translucent plastic bag collected the catheter drippings.

Michael slid his hand down from my arm to my hand. He held it tight, his warmth doing nothing to quell the coldness in my palm. Together we stood shoulder to shoulder at the foot of the bed.

Robyn's mother hadn't shifted her gaze from her daughter's face when I pulled back the curtain. "She called me just before she left," June said, her eyes still locked on Robyn's. "It must have been her third blind date in a row." She shook her head bitterly. "I warned her, told her she was seeing too many men, too many strangers. That it would all catch up with her one day."

I recalled Robyn bragging about a stockbroker. But now I knew she'd been lying. That she'd been seeing more men than just the stockbroker. That she'd been playing with Match.com like it was some kind of game that didn't involve real people, real strangers.

Her mother sniffled, the tall, brown-haired, middle-aged woman fighting back the tears as best she could. But I knew it had to be a losing battle. She inhaled and set her right hand on Robyn's forehead, running trembling fingers down through dirty-blonde hair.

Set beside the bed was a vital functions monitor. Its steady, mechanical up-and-down green line represented Robyn's heart rate. It reminded me of the one that had been attached to Molly before she died.

"Early this morning," June went on, "I was woken up by a phone call. It was the police. They'd responded to a 9-1-1 coming from the Cocoa Motel near the airport. They found my Robyn curled up on the motel room floor. She was beaten, bleeding, half-unconscious…my poor Robyn." She paused, hesitating, crying. "Two of her ribs are broken, plus one finger on her right hand. A clump of hair was pulled out of her head." She choked on the next words. "What kind of animal does something like this, Rebecca?"

I knew full well what kind of animal did that. Why was it so hard to believe in a benevolent God, but so easy to believe in the presence of real evil?

"What about the police?" I said. "Do they have any clue who could have done this?"

Michael squeezed my hand, like I'd just asked June if the cops suspected Whalen.

She dried her eyes, turned slowly around to face Michael and me. "Robyn was able to give a decent description before they sedated her."

"Cops get a name?" Michael pressed.

"It's a young man, posing as a salesman on a business trip." Not Whalen, then. "Makes contact over an online dating service like that computer 'Match' thing, arranges a date, flies into town, wines and dines, gets the date to bed. Then he does something like this."

She turned back to her daughter and ran an open hand over her body as if to better demonstrate her point.

"The police establish any kind of trail, June?" Michael continued probing. "Any kind of a lead on his whereabouts?"

"He's already flown out. He's operating under so many aliases they don't know where to start." Biting her lip, she looked over my shoulder at Michael. "Albany Police claim that it's an FBI problem now. That they'll get to him soon enough."

"I know they will," I whispered. But I wasn't sure I believed it.

Soon enough…

June tried to plant a semblance of a smile on her face. "The police said that it took some guts for Robyn to cooperate the way she did, especially with that animal still out there. That the reason this man is able to get away with so many attacks is that most of his victims are too ashamed to come to the police."

"Or too scared," I added, feeling a boulder-sized lump in my throat. I knew about fear's crippling paralysis. Once more my eyes caught the monitor, the thin, ceaseless, up-and-down green line.

June stood up straight. "Rebecca," she said, "can I talk with you privately?"

Michael let go of my hand. "I'll go get some coffee," he offered, stepping around the curtain.

After a few weighted seconds I could see that June was crying again. I went to her, put my arm around her, my eyes peeled on the ever-still Robyn. "What is it?"

"My baby," she whispered. "My Robyn. She didn't use protection. Rather, *he…*"

I knew what she was trying to say. It hit me like a sledgehammer to the gut.

"They retrieved seminal fluid during an internal," she explained, before bursting into tears.

Just what had Robyn been thinking?

I couldn't help but wonder if she'd been sleeping with lots of men while using nothing to prevent pregnancy or worse, contracting some horrible STD. But then, what if this creep forced it on her before she had the chance to even speak of protection?

"Have the doctors run any further tests?" I asked.

At first, June said nothing. Then she set her cold, wet hand on mine. "Robyn is six weeks pregnant."

Chapter 40

AT MY URGING WE DROVE FROM THE ALBANY MEDICAL Center in the direction of the South Pearl Street precinct. We might have been riding in silence but my thoughts screamed at me. My mind kept shifting from the horror of Robyn's rape to the shock of her pregnancy. *Was it possible that she had no idea about it?* I'd never before been pregnant, but I did know that by the time six weeks went by, you had to be suspecting something. Your body went through changes. Your inner voice spoke to you. I could only wonder just who the father was. The stockbroker? Or someone she met weeks before him? I wasn't entirely sure of the timeline or the course of events in Robyn's dangerous love life.

I spoke up as we approached State Street and asked Michael to make a pit stop at the School of Art on the way to the police. In light of Robyn's condition and Whalen's unexpected homecoming, I wanted to leave a note on the front door explaining that the place would be closed for the rest of the week due to a personal emergency. I also wanted to change the answering service message to reflect the same message.

When it was done, I got back in the truck and Michael pulled out onto the main road, heading farther into the city. When we arrived at the APD, I carried the *Smell* canvas with me. We learned that Detective Harris wasn't in, but that same gray-haired watch commander was at the counter to greet us. He said that if we wanted to wait, Harris would be back within the half hour. I knew then that I should have called the detective, let him know we were coming. But it was too late now.

The precinct smelled bad. Not altogether unlike that sewer-like smell I recalled from the house in the woods. The watch commander must have noticed our sour faces because he pinched his own nostrils together, said, "Plumber's on his way. Old cast-iron pipes in this building just can't keep up with the flow anymore… If you know what I mean."

I nodded.

"Tell you what. Jack's Diner is just across the street. Excellent home cooking, real good coffee. Why don't you wait for Harris there? When he comes back, I'll have him give you a call right away." The big man smiled.

"Sounds good, Sergeant," Michael said.

"Course it is," the gray-haired cop said, waving his hand rapidly in front of his face, as if it were possible to wave away the stench. "Stay here much longer you'll lose your cookies."

I asked the watch commander if I could leave the painting behind.

"Sure thing," he answered. "We could use a little culturing around here." Then he said, "Hey, John Grisham, you got a new book comin' out?"

"Workin' on it," Michael said, not without a grin.

We departed the APD, headed across the street to the diner, where we sat ourselves in a corner booth that overlooked South Pearl Street and the red brick police station. Michael ordered us coffee and toasted hard rolls with butter. I managed to drink the coffee, but only picked at the hard roll.

We sat and waited for Harris's call.

And waited.

When my cell phone chimed, I nearly jumped out of the booth.

Taking charge, Michael picked up the phone, answered. While he listened, he laser-beamed his eyes into mine. "Right away, Detective," he said, hanging up.

He slid a five and two ones from his pocket, tossed them onto the table.

"What did Harris say?" I asked.

"He wants to see us now. He's got news."

I felt my pulse race.

Whalen.

"This time we tell him about the texts. Agreed?" Michael insists.

"That's why we're here," I say.

Chapter 41

JUST LIKE YESTERDAY WHEN WE FIRST MET WITH HIM inside his private office, Harris politely asked us to sit. Only this time, instead of seating himself behind his desk, he perched himself on the desk's edge before us, one foot hanging off, the other planted firmly on the floor. Today he was wearing a tan blazer over a white button-down, no tie. The bulge under the left breast pocket told me he stored a pair of reading glasses inside the interior pocket. He crossed his arms over chest. Over his right shoulder I could see that the previous calendar day had been neatly X'd off in blue ballpoint. The precinct still stunk like a sewer. But no one mentioned a word about it.

"The paintings," he began to explain. "Just for your peace of mind, I thought you might like to know that thus far anyway, the Albany labs see nothing to indicate Whalen had any kind of contact with them whatsoever. My guess is that the only people to lay hands on them—besides present company of course—is your student, Francis, perhaps his mother, maybe your partner, Robyn. But no Whalen."

I shot a glance up at Michael where he stood beside my chair. His eyebrows were raised just like the detective's.

I shook my head. "Not a chance," I insisted. "What, you thought Franny might somehow be working with Whalen? No way. Franny would never do anything to hurt anyone. He also knows right from wrong, and Whalen is definitely wrong."

"Francis having direct contact with Whalen would certainly answer the question of how the artist is able to paint your memories."

The tug in my stomach intensified. I felt like all the oxygen in the room had been sucked out through the vents, leaving only the foul odor.

"What about Whalen?" Michael pressed. "Did you make contact with his parole officer?"

The detective looked up. "I did," he confirmed. "Whalen has very recently been employed at the Hollywood Car Wash on Central in the west end. According to his parole officer, Whalen listed the joint as his first choice of employment."

"A creep like Whalen gets to choose?" Michael posed.

Harris perked up his brow. "A creep like Whalen gets to choose a state-funded dentist, a state-funded medical plan that best suits his needs, and even which bank or credit union he gets to build a retirement nest egg at. This is the progressive-minded New York State, Mr. Hoffman, and ex-cons like Whalen enjoy quite a few rights. One of those rights is place of employment, so long as that place is acceptable to the parole board. Certainly the Hollywood Car Wash passes muster."

The Hollywood Car Wash. A vision of the place flashed through my head. I made a once-a-week visit to the place to wash Molly's Cabriolet. Whether it needed it or not. Of all the businesses in Albany, the parole board has to set him up with a job there? My God, had I *seen* him there?

Before I could sort through the faces I'd encountered at the car wash, Harris went on. "He lives in a halfway house on Clinton, not a block away from work. Fully registered with sex offenders, as you well know. Shows up for the early and evening meals per state regs, wears a monitoring bracelet around his right ankle. It's house arrest from that point on, until work starts the next morning. Lights out at ten. From all appearances, Whalen is a model parolee—a system success story."

"So what're you trying to say, detective?" Michael posed. "That there's no reason to suggest Whalen has been acting in any way suspicious? You don't see him as a threat?"

Harris shrugged. "Not an immediate threat, anyway," he said. But then, raising his right hand, pointing an extended index finger at the painting I'd brought into the office with me: "I remain, however, more than a little curious about Franny the artist."

The Hollywood Car Wash…I can't let this coincidence go unnoticed. And then I remembered the old man.

"Wait just a minute," I broke in. "I had my car washed on Tuesday morning. I almost always have my car washed on Tuesday mornings."

Michael and Harris turned their attention to me as if an alarm had just gone off.

"I had my car washed and an older man dried it. The Hollywood Car Wash on Central. A short white-bearded man with a head full of white hair. He smiled at me, spoke to me. I gave him a five-dollar tip because I felt sorry for him for having to work in a car wash."

Harris looked at Michael. Michael looked at me.

"I can only assume that's him," Harris said. "Did he give you any reason to suggest he knew you? Did he use your name?"

My head was spinning. "No," I said. "The man didn't say much of anything."

"What made you go to the car wash in the first place?"

"I get Molly's car washed every Tuesday morning, whether it needs it or not. It's what Molly always did. Every Tuesday, rain or shine or snow. It was her ritual."

"Dollars to doughnuts," Harris said, "if that was in fact Whalen, he knew you were coming. He would have planned it that way."

"I'd never seen him there before."

"That's because you weren't aware of him until recently."

An explosion came from outside precinct walls. Thunder. Loud enough to cause all three of us to glance at the far wall, as if there was a window to see out of.

"Tell him about the texts," Michael insisted.

I looked up at my ex-husband, then shifted to Harris. "Someone unknown has been sending me texts over the period of a few months."

Harris raised his eyebrows. "What did the messages say?"

"Usually just my name at first. *Rebecca*. My name spelled in lower case. On occasion it would be another word, 'remember.'"

He jotted down some notes in a small notebook he stored in his shirt pocket.

"You saw him in the car wash on Tuesday," Harris recalled. "Did his face ring any kind of bell whatsoever?"

I felt my stomach drop. Did the face of the nice old man match the face of the rapist in the ViCAP database? "Not at all," I said. "Not with all that hair. I guess I might have seen the same white-haired man there a dozen times before over the course of a few months. But only on Tuesday did I feel the need to pay attention to him."

"The texts," Harris went on. "What was the number left on your caller ID?"

"Like she said," Michael spoke for me. "Unknown Caller."

Harris transferred himself behind the cluttered desk. He shifted his eyes back to me.

"I'm going to check into the possibility that Whalen could be texting you, Rebecca. If he's got the money for a cell phone, he's allowed a cell phone. Simple as that. You save the messages?"

"He's been in the joint for thirty years," Michael interjected. "How would he know how to use a cell phone? How would he know how to text?"

"A five-minute tutorial will solve that problem," Harris answered. "Hell, I'll bet they teach it in the life skills classes they give the cons before their release." Then, focusing once more on me: "So what's the deal, Rebecca, did you save those texts?"

I told him I had.

He asked to see my phone.

I handed it to him from across the desk.

"You have a security code?" Harris asked.

I shook my head, frowned. "Too lazy. Too stupid."

"Learn to use one," he said. "Cell phones are easy to lose. People steal them, use them. You pay the bill. But what's worse, is that if you have your address stored on it, and some personal pictures, your social networks, somebody can easily infiltrate your entire life history, not to mention your home."

My stomach began to cave in on itself. The nausea was settling back in. The world was a very dangerous place. With and without Whalen.

The detective pulled his reading glasses from inside his jacket pocket, slipped them on. Then he flipped open the phone, thumbed some buttons. Although I couldn't see exactly what he was getting at, I knew he had to be looking at the messages. I knew he was trying to get something from their accompanying information. Or in this case, noninformation.

After a time, he looked up. "Verizon is your carrier I see," he said, handing the phone back to me.

"You're not going to confiscate it?"

"I have your number. Verizon cell phone records are easy enough to access."

"How is it Whalen would be able to block his caller ID?" Michael interjected. It was a question both of us wanted to ask.

"You want to block your ID and number when making a call or a text," he explained, "you just punch star-six-seven before dialing the desired telephone number. You want to unlock your ID, punch in star-eight-two. It's as simple as that and totally legal."

"Whalen would know how to do that right out of prison?" Michael pressed.

Harris nodded emphatically. "Again, Mr. Hoffman, a simple tutorial or classroom lesson. Or maybe he learned it all in prison via the cable television or the computer."

"Jesus, prisoners have Internet access?" I asked.

"Yes. Limited and monitored access. But yes, they have the right to go online. Only seems normal that a man who's about to be paroled would look up info on how to use a cell phone."

Harris was making sense, as frightening as it seemed. Then I remembered something. "There was another woman there at the Hollywood Car Wash. A well-dressed woman who was driving a Mercedes-Benz. She was upset because she had lost her cell phone while her car was being washed."

Harris bit down on his bottom lip, bobbed his head. "That could explain it," he allowed. "It's possible Whalen is stealing cell phones, using them to text you." He opened a bottom desk drawer, pulled out a phone book, and slapped it heavily onto the desktop.

"Wow, a real old-fashioned phone book," Michael pointed out.

"They still make them, believe it or not," Harris said, his eyes glued to the black-and-white pages as he flipped them. "I refuse to give in to every modern convenience just because it saves a split second or two."

"You're a man of honor and integrity, detective," Michael quipped.

"Thanks for noticing," Harris said, pressing an extended index finger on the number he was searching for. "I'm going to call the Hollywood Car Wash, find out if they've had a rash of lost mobile phones over the past few months." Looking back at me, he continued, "If that's everything, I need to get on this right away."

I stood, a little out of balance.

"Detective," I said. "I just have one question."

"What is it?"

"Do you truly suspect that Franny might have something to do with all this? Something other than what's going on in his mind?"

The detective bit his bottom lip again. "I honestly don't know what to think. I'm still having trouble comprehending his apparent accuracy in depicting your memories. On one hand, we have a paroled Whalen who might be sending you texts; who might have tried to break into your Brunswick home; who might have left a photograph of you and your sister on the home's porch floor; who might in fact be stalking you. On the other hand, we have an autistic savant who is able to accurately paint your memories and dreams, as though you were dictating them to him."

"But where do Whalen and Francis connect?" Michael demanded.

Harris filled his cheeks with air and slowly released it. "Well, Rebecca has already told me that the black-and-white photo of her and Molly matches one of Franny's paintings. That raises the possibility that Whalen and Francis might have had access to the same photograph."

"Not at the same time," I said.

"We don't know that," Harris said. "Not yet."

I told him that it's not unusual for an autistic savant to be able to tap into portions of the brain that normal people can't even hope for. It seemed possible to me that Franny's talent might very well include the ability to see inside my head. Or at the very least, to be able to see the future.

"OK," Harris uttered, a heavy note of cynicism in his voice. "I'll take your word for it, for now. But if it turns out Whalen's and Francis's prints are on that black-and-white photograph of you and your sister, it'll only please me to pay the Scaramuzzis a little visit."

"Franny has been through enough already," I explained.

"How so?"

"The other day I got in his face, yelled at him. Like you, I'd started to believe there could be something more to the paintings than just an active imagination. An accurate imagination, that is."

I started toward the door, until something else hit me.

"My partner and best friend," I said. "Robyn Painter. Are you aware of the assault on her last night, Detective Harris?"

I felt my heart pound when I said it. Harris was helping me, but I almost felt angry with him for not having mentioned it already. The look on his face was hard, angry, tight-lipped. I knew then that he knew about what had happened at that motel.

"Wish I could say we had a better lead on the creep who did it. FBI is taking over the investigation. Your friend, Robyn…she's not the only one."

"I'm aware of that." I swallowed.

Michael took my hand, gave it a squeeze.

Harris picked up the phone, held it in his hand. "Again, I'll ask you to call me if something else comes up."

"What about the paintings?" Michael asked.

"I'm going to hang onto them along with the black-and-white pic of you and your sister, Rebecca. In the meantime I'm going to check into these texts, see if they really do somehow lead to Whalen."I have another painting," I said, nodding toward the canvas where it was leaned up against Michael's chair.

Harris glanced at it. "That's the house?" he asked under his breath.

"Yes."

"I'm so very sorry."

I turned away from him, made my way out the door, back into the foul-smelling air.

Chapter 42

WE LEFT THE CITY AND DROVE IN THE DIRECTION OF my apartment.

Michael set his hand on my leg. "Let's skip town," he said. "Why don't we pack a quick bag, head down to New York for the night. Just like old times. We can get a room at the Gramercy Park, head out to Les Halles for steak frites, maybe a hit a bar or two. Just like we used to do."

It sounded very appealing. Getting out of town for a night. God it sounded good.

"Do you think it's a good idea to leave Robyn?"

"She needs rest, Bec. Not visitors. Besides, she's got her mother and we'll be back tomorrow afternoon."

Michael was making sense. But there was just one more obstacle.

"What do we use for money?"

He tossed me a grin. "Got a few bucks put away."

"You robbed a convenience store and got away with it. Congratulations."

"I've been selling the occasional news piece," he offered. "Strictly online fluff stuff."

We pulled into the apartment complex. Michael parked the truck in my designated spot. As we walked around the building to the terrace, I saw that the sky was blackening, the clouds gathering with some speed. There was also a significant wind. Definitely a storm coming.

Outside the apartment door a team of blue-uniformed maintenance workers were raking leaves. No one seemed to notice me.

I unlocked the door. Stepping inside the apartment, I felt suddenly lighter. Even the thought of heading down to New York for a night was enough to send a wave of optimism through my body.

Michael closed the door behind me. "So do I have a date for Les Halles tonight or what?"

"Make the reservation," I said, turning to him, giving him a quick peck on the cheek. "I'm going to wash up, pack an overnight bag, and we're gone."

He smiled, hugged me tight. "No worries, Bec."

"It's all good," I lied. True or false, it felt good to simply say it.

As I made my way through the hall to the bathroom, I heard the sound of distant thunder.

Chapter 43

TURNING ON BOTH THE HOT AND COLD WATER, I looked at my face in the mirror before attempting to wash it.

Looked into *our* faces, I should say. Molly's and mine.

Sometimes when I see my reflected self, I wonder if Molly would have looked the same, if her ageing process would have mimicked my own. And then I tell myself that of course it would have. Though how precisely? I wonder if she would have acquired the same horizontal lines in her forehead, the same little bit of extra skin under the chin, the newly emerging crow's-feet framing the eyes, the subtle hint of gray in the otherwise dirty-blonde hair.

Essentially, I wonder if she would be me.

I felt the vibration against my thigh. Drying my hands, I pulled the cell phone from my jeans pocket and flipped it open.

Another text.

My heart raced and my mouth went dry.

I thumbed it open.

Cry, cry, cry, you naughty kitten.

Tears built up behind my eyeballs. I never bothered with checking the caller ID. I knew who the caller was. I simply closed the phone and slipped it back into my jeans pocket. Breathing in and out, I turned off the water.

Then a loud bang, like someone closing a kitchen drawer. It gave my heart a start. Following that, a slight commotion, muffled voices, my bedroom door slamming shut.

Michael.

I wanted to call out his name, but I couldn't. My hand trembled as I opened the bathroom door and went out into the hall. It took forever to reach the bedroom. But when I did, a loud burst of thunder rattled my bones.

When I opened the bedroom door, I knew immediately that we would not be going to New York City.

Chapter 44

THE REALITY OF THE SITUATION DIDN'T IMMEDIATELY register.

It just looked like Michael was lying on the bed taking a quick nap before we hit the road for the 140-mile drive south to New York. But a fraction of a second later, the fog lifted and the real scene came to light: his shirt ripped off, his mouth gagged with duct tape, his hands hastily duct-taped together at the wrists, his legs bound together at the ankles.

He was still, eyes shut, body lying fetal on the bed.

I stood there paralyzed. Stood there staring at Michael, one side of his face pressed into the pillow, the exposed half lit from the light that leaked in through the open window.

The bedroom was as still as an empty church. My copy of *Mockingbird* had been tossed onto the floor by the bed. I stood petrified, my feet planted in concrete. I gazed up and down at Michael's naked chest with a kind of dumb, horrified curiosity. A small cut had been made just below his right nipple. A thin line of blood trickled from it, ran down along his ribcage. The dark hair on his head was mussed up. A thin streak of blood ran down the center of his forehead. I knew then he'd been hit over the head with a blunt object.

I knew I could not be alone; someone else was inside the apartment besides Michael and me. The ashtray smell. It was a familiar smell. I knew that smell as well as I knew myself.

I had no idea how long I'd been standing inside that open door, just staring at the bound image of my ex-husband. A half second maybe. Or a full minute. Fear warped time, bent it the same way it crippled my insides.

For me, the present moment no longer contained any logic or proportion. I knew I had to do something. What I wanted to do was lift my feet, put one foot in front of the other. I wanted to unbind Michael, rescue him.

But I just stood there doing nothing.

My hesitation must have been exactly what Whalen was counting on when he opened my closet door and stepped out into the bedroom.

Chapter 45

MY AWAKENING WAS AS PAINFUL AS IT WAS SUDDEN.

Michael was gone. Disappeared.

Aside from the sting in my head, his absence was the first thing that caught my attention.

There remained only my cell, which had been removed from my jeans pocket and set on the wooden floor directly before my eyes. There was a throbbing pain in my head and an egg-sized lump protruding above my right eye. I touched the lump with the fingers on my right hand only to pull them back quick from the sting.

For a moment, I didn't quite know where I was. Rather, I knew where I was, but I couldn't be sure if I had entered into one of my vivid dreams. *Had my dreaming progressed from hearing his voice to actually hearing the man; seeing him; smelling him; feeling him?* I breathed, tried my hardest to calm myself; tried to focus on ending the dream, going back to sleep.

I wanted it to be morning.

I wanted to wake up to sunshine, to my routine. But every time I closed my eyes, I opened them again to the reality of the moment. All objects inside my periphery were blurry, distorted, depth-of-field spinning, pulsing like an out-of-control video camera.

Pushing myself up off an exposed hardwood floor, I sat up and felt a great weight inside my head. The throw rug that had covered the floor was gone. I saw the empty place that Michael had occupied in the bed. All that remained now were the crumpled bedsheets, the discarded shirt tossed to the floor.

I pulled the bedroom door open, ran out into the hall. That's when the cell phone exploded in loud, bursting pulses. Whalen must have adjusted the ringer setting.

Running back into the bedroom, I picked up the phone and put it to my ear. But no sound came through the earpiece. In the place of a voice came a notice for a new text.

I thumbed OK on the keypad.

The text appeared on the radiant face of the phone.

Do not run, little kitten. Do not call the police. Do not speak. Break the rules and Michael dies. Cry, cry, cry.

"Where is he?! What have you done with him?!" I screamed into the phone—stupidly, forgetting Whalen's message had come to me by text. Heart pulsing inside my throat, I waited for an answer. A voice. But then I remembered to pull the phone away from my ear, stare down at the screen. The answer revealed itself in the form of another text.

Little kitten broke the rules. Cry. Cry. Cry.

Chapter 46

I FELT ON THE VERGE OF FAINTING. MY BREATHING became rapid and forced.

I made my way back into the bathroom, yanked up the shade and stared out the window onto the parking lot. Blue and black clouds filled the sky. The occasional flicker of distant lightning lit them up. The usual cars were parked in the lot, including Michael's truck. From where I stood it was impossible for me to see my Cabriolet.

Turning, I held the phone back up to my face, staring down at the display panel. I thumbed the command that would reveal Whalen's number. The caller ID came back, "Restricted Number." With trembling fingers I began to dial 9-1-1.

But I stopped myself.

I stared out into the thickening darkness and the silence of the apartment. *What if the police come to my home? Whalen must be watching me. He must have been watching me now for weeks, months. What will he do when he sees the police car? What kind of revenge will he take out on Michael?*

What kind of revenge was he already *doling out because I'd disobeyed him? He said Michael would die if I spoke. But I screamed. I. Fucking. Screamed. Why did I scream?!*

All strength seeped out of me. My hand and the phone it gripped fell to the side. I had no idea which way to turn for help. Not without getting Michael killed in the process.

I sensed someone behind me.

I knew he was there before I actually saw him. Something inside my brain went click. My eyes rolled back into their sockets. The floor beneath me turned to mud. I turned around, but did so in slow motion. I screamed, but the sound of my voice was like an old vinyl record played at slow speed. When my eyes connected with his, I felt all oxygen leave my lungs. It was as if I'd been kicked in the stomach by an invisible booted foot.

There he was: the source of my fear; the author of my texts.

Tomorrow will mark thirty years exactly since you abducted Molly and me... You are one day early...

He was the old man from the Hollywood Car Wash. His was the face from ViCAP. He was the monster from my dreams. He was shaven clean now, and what had been long white hair was now a bald scalp. His face was gaunt, cheeks sallow, chin protruding. His pallor was chalk-pale. Dark round eyes made the paleness all the whiter.

Now for certain I remembered the face. I remembered the man; the monster.

I took in all these details with every single one of my senses as he approached me in the hall of my apartment, dressed in the worn work boots and the blue uniform of the apartment complex maintenance crew. Standing there I could only wonder how he managed to get Michael out of there without anyone spotting him. He must have wrapped Michael up in the rug, dragged him out the front door like a piece of furniture. There were always people moving in and out of these apartments. Who would notice?

In one hand he held a needle and syringe. In the other, a pistol. He stared into my eyes as I began to feel myself losing all sense of balance.

"My other little kitten is gone," he sobbed, in a gruff, high-pitched moan.

I knew precisely who he was referring to. I never had to think about it.

"Yes," I choked out. "Molly died."

"Cry, cry, cry," he whispered, his eyes tearing, his bottom lip protruding out in pout position. "Cry, cry, cry."

He hadn't yet touched me with the tip of that needle before I passed out.

Chapter 47

MOLLY ENTERS THE HOUSE IN THE WOODS BEFORE ME.
She is not bothered by the smell any more than she is bothered by
the creepy feel of the spiderwebs that hang from the ceilings and the
walls. The interior is trashed, broken furniture scattered all about
what was once an open living room. Looking all around me, I see
that most of the walls have been opened up, probably with claw
hammers, almost all of the copper piping and wiring torn away by
scrap hunters. There's an old chandelier that hangs from the ceiling,
its bulbs gone along with any crystals that had once hung from it.

And that smell. It's just as bad inside as it is outside.

"Come on," Molly says. "I want to show you the upstairs."

Out the corner of my eye, I make out the staircase that leads up
to a second floor. Its treads are no longer level, but have canted to
the side and sunk down at the back. Just looking at them frightens
me so that I can't imagine stepping on them, placing weight upon
them. But Molly isn't the least bit afraid. She heads to the stairs and,
in the home's semidarkness, begins climbing them, one at a time.

I follow.

As we ascend the staircase in near pitch darkness, I begin to
smell a new odor. It's the same smell you get inside an old abandoned
barn. The smell of cats and their urine. As we come to the second-

floor landing, a black cat scurries out from a room at the far end of the hall, runs right past us.

"Hi, Blacky," Mol says, as the cat leaps back down the steps.

A choked laugh. "Obviously you two are acquainted," I say.

"We're old friends," she adds.

"Look at all this room, Bec," she goes on. "There're two rooms apiece for us."

I go no farther than the first bedroom. There's an old bare mattress set out on the floor, its rusted springs sticking out of the holes. There are dark spatter stains on the walls. What could've made them? All I can think of is blood and the boogeyman, and I force my mind away from that.

There's an exposed lightbulb that hangs down from a wire. If it were not for the sunlight that sneaks in through the cracked double-hung windows, the place would be pitch black.

I find myself shaking. I'm having trouble breathing. Something bad has happened here. Something bad enough for the place to have been abandoned.

"I'm going back down, Mol," I say through chattering teeth. "I don't like it up here."

"Don't like it?" she says, running from room to room, jumping up and down on the bare mattresses. "It's all ours!"

I turn back for the stairs. That's when I hear the front door slam shut.

THE WOODS

Chapter 48

THE CELL PHONE WOKE ME FROM DRUG-INDUCED sleep. I raised myself up to my knees, scraped away the wet pine needles that were stuck to my right cheek. I'd opened my eyes onto a darkness broken only by a tiny flashing red light embedded inside the plastic phone casing. Climbing onto my knees, I reached for the phone, opened it.

I was wet and shivering. I was also dizzy, wobbly. Out of instinct, I pressed the phone to my ear, listened for a voice. But then it dawned on me that there would be no voice.

Setting the phone flat in the palm of my hand, I peered down at the illuminated screen. Opening and closing my eyes, I tried hard to focus. There was a message there.

Do you luv Michael, little kitten?

I thumbed in an answer. Pounded it in.

Do not hurt him.

It took forever to type in the letters, my eyes straining to focus through the haze of sedation in the light rain.

Another text came through.

Cry, cry, cry, little kitten.

No choice but to play the game. That meant telling the truth.

I luv Michael.

I awaited Whalen's reply. It came quickly, as though the text had been prepared ahead of time and copied in.

Flashlight is at your feet. Pick it up and turn it on, little kitten.

Still on my knees, I reached out with my free hand, probing the wet mix of pine needles, leaves, and raw earth with bare fingers until I located the flashlight. It was heavy in my hand. Its light showed that Whalen had dropped me inside a patch of thick woods. The monster had drugged me, hauled me out to some remote area, and dropped my unconscious body inside it. Somewhere wild, somewhere dense with cover. Somewhere cold.

Another text.

Go to pictures, little kitten.

I thumbed the menu key. A second screen appeared, this one offering eight options. The first for recent calls, the second for personal phone book, the third for games. And so on. I fingered the number 6 on the keypad. A picture appeared. A man who had been bound with silver duct tape. A man of medium build forced down on his knees. Like me, he seemed to be kneeling inside a thick patch of woods, while a bright white light shined on him, as if coming from a set of headlights. In the picture I could see that the man's hair was dark, thick. He was bare-chested. The mustached face had been covered with separate strips of duct tape, one covering the eyes, the other covering the mouth, leaving only an exposed nose through which to breathe.

The tape acted like a mask. But I didn't need to view the entire face to recognize Michael.

I wiped the beaded rainwater from the small screen, moving on to the next picture. Michael was still down on his knees. Only this time, he wasn't inside a patch of woods. He was inside a building or a house. Down inside a basement. He was down on his knees on a hard-packed gravel and dirt floor. Stone and cinderblock walls surrounded him. He was bathed in harsh white light, just like in the previous picture. This time, probably from an exposed lightbulb.

I knew that basement, knew what had happened there. To Molly and me.

I dropped the phone, coughed up bile. It filled my mouth, burned my throat. Spitting it out, I deeply inhaled cool wet air. I was afraid to pick the phone back up; afraid of what came next. I'd already seen enough.

I had no choice but to pick the phone back up. No choice but to keep on looking. It seemed to take every ounce of my will, but I thumbed to the next picture and drew my eyes to the screen.

This time I saw myself. Rather, not only myself, but Michael and me seated on the couch in my apartment, sipping wine. The picture appeared to have been snapped from just outside the apartment window.

I depressed the keypad, moved on to the next picture. And the next, and the next...

Me, knapsack in one hand, one of Franny's canvases in the other, moving toward my Cabriolet inside an empty downtown Broadway parking garage; me running for the Cabriolet; me jumping behind the wheel; me standing on the porch of my parents' home, staring out onto the woods and Mount Desolation beyond them; me holding the black-and-white photo of Molly and me in my hand as I sat down onto the porch, pressed my back up against the clapboard wall...

I guess I wasn't nuts after all. Whalen had been following me all along.

More photos appeared. Black-and-white images.

Molly and me when we were no more than three, running in the backyard behind our farmhouse. A color shot of Molly and me waiting for the school bus in our St. Catherine's elementary school white-and-blue-checkered uniform skirts. Molly and me as preteens playing one of our nightly games of flashlight tag in the tall grass behind our home on a hot summer's night. Molly in her bed asleep, me undressing in my bedroom—both photos no doubt shot from outside our windows, where Whalen must have perched himself on the porch overhang.

All those years ago…

Chapter 49

THE PHONE PULSED IN MY HAND. THUMBING SEND I read:

Run away, little kitten. I'm going to chase u now. You remember the game. Flashlight tag. Cry, cry, cry.

I peered at the radiant display hoping that I would wake up from a dream. But this wasn't a dream. It was the past relived. This was Whalen chasing Molly and me through the woods, again.

I closed the phone, shoved it in my pocket, looked up at the sky and saw only darkness and clouds illuminated by the distant flicker of lightning. I had to find a way to deal, get a grip.

I started by gripping the flashlight and aiming it dead ahead.

Chapter 50

THE FLASHLIGHT LIT UP A STAND OF BRUSH, VINES, AND trees directly in front of me. Making my way through that thick stuff would have been impossible. Shifting clockwise, I began to pivot on the balls of my feet like a dancer pirouetting in slow motion. I kept this rotation up, keeping the shining light out ahead of me, until I recognized a narrow foot or deer trail that cut through the thick woods. Probably the same trail that had been here since Molly and I were girls.

I was doing my best to think clearly, without panic. Doing my best not to lose my mind. If ever I wished Molly by my side, now was the time. I had to force myself to think like her. What would she do?

She'd follow the path and keep moving. I was determined to do the same thing.

She'd get going down that trail.

But that's when things began to go rapidly south: the flashlight began to fade.

The beam quickly faded to a kind of yellowish half-light. My pulse picked up. I opened my mouth, allowing some of the rain to fall onto my tongue.

What would I do without the light? What would I do in the pitch dark? How would I find the house? How would I find Michael?

I shook the flashlight, but it was useless, wasted motion. Common sense told me to use whatever available power I had left in the flashlight to enter onto the trailhead and get the hell away from this place. I aimed the dim light out ahead of me, making my way across the clearing in what I could only pray was Michael's direction.

I was standing at the edge of the chosen trail when the flashlight went dead.

Chapter 51

RAIN BEGAN TO POUR DOWN IN SHEETS OF PAINFUL, icy bullets. The heavy cloud cover surrounded the hillside like a vapor ring. Directly before me came intermittent explosions of lightning. Without them the darkness of the woods would have been absolute and impenetrable. Because of the cloud cover, no stars shined up above. No moonbeams penetrated the low-lying mist and fog.

I was still stalled at the trailhead, working up the courage to begin my blind journey. I had spun to peer back behind me when another quick shot of lightning struck the ground somewhere off in the distance. Its thunder pounded and reverberated. But its flash illuminated a field that was visible through a thin line of trees.

Our field, and my parents' house at the far end of it. I was looking directly at my parents' property.

I turned back around to the trailhead. It was a trail I knew. What had seemed like a dream was now painfully real. Whalen had kidnapped Michael and me, somehow dragged us up to Mount Desolation. Michael was inside that old house in the woods. He was tied up, held hostage in the basement. If I didn't get to him before Whalen got to me, he would die. Or maybe we would both die anyway.

I inhaled a deep breath, exhaled, tried to get my head together, tried to think logically, without fear or emotion clouding my judgment. Another distant lightning strike, then another—just enough light to show me the first ten yards or so of the path I was about to tread. It would lead downhill. Downhill toward the house.

Though I knew that it wouldn't be purely downhill. Mount Desolation wasn't really a mountain at all. It was made up of several large hills that crested and dipped before the flat, heavily wooded land finally took over. That was where I'd come to know that terrible house in the woods.

I was a blind woman forced to move by touch, one foot before the other, the rain coming down stronger now against my face and head, running down my scrunched brow in streaks. I knew it was possible to use the light from the cell phone to illuminate my way, one step at a time. But I needed to save every bit of battery charge I had left. I had no choice but to move around in the darkness without the use of my eyes.

Branches slapped me in the face and my eyes teared up. Big tears fell and mixed with the rain on my face. I tried to stay on the narrow trail. I was blind, trying to stay free and clear of the brush and the trees; trying to do it by touch, with arms and hands extended out in front of me while I moved at a slow, frustrating trot.

Another lightning bolt revealed a landscape of thick, dripping growth. The sight of it lasted only a split second. Pine trees and mulberry bushes intermixed with birches and oaks. Still another bolt revealed something else—something scattering before me. Something alive, quick, and fleeting.

At first I thought it might be a dog. Maybe a deer. Instinct told me to drop to my knees while gripping the flashlight, holding it out before me. It was my only available weapon. Lightning struck.

Thunder exploded. The impact took my breath away, shook the ground at my feet. Lightning restored my sense of sight. It allowed me to spot the monster, if only for an instant. That single instant was all it took for me to know the truth.

Whalen blocked the trail.

Whalen, head shaved, dressed in dark clothing, smiling, eyes covered with goggles. Green-tinted eyes. Green-tinted, mechanical, night-vision eyes. He stood in the center of the narrow trail, heavy rain washing over his lean body.

All oxygen escaped my lungs. Blindness returned. But not for long.

More lightning lit up the night sky. Another view of the path came and went with the speed of a heartbeat.

Now the path was clear.

Like the lightning, Whalen had vanished in an instant.

Now you see the devil. Now you don't.

Chapter 52

I STUFFED THE NOW USELESS FLASHLIGHT INTO MY pant waist, handle first. With every step I took along the trail in the darkness came a branch slap to the face, a tree trunk to the thigh, a boulder to the shin. I caught a thorn from a thick bush that hung over the trail; it tore into my jeans, penetrating the skin on my lower calf. I knew I was cut. Not because I could feel the sting. But because I could feel the blood trickling down the calf muscle, warm and wet, the thick consistency not at all like the cold October rain.

It was a struggle to get anywhere in the dark. Five minutes of walking and stumbling, and I had managed to cover no more than thirty or forty feet. Whether or not I was maintaining a straight line was a mystery to me. I might as well have been crawling.

The lightning had stopped; no more flashes of light. The only way to continue the blind trek was to drop down onto hands and knees, feel my way along the trail the same way an animal might do it: by touch, by smell, by sound.

From down on all fours, I crawled over the smooth rocks and mud-covered gravel toward the sound of water. Not rainwater falling from the sky, but stream water running heavily into a pool. I knew the pool from my childhood. It had to be the same one. The more I crawled the louder, more forceful it became. I knew the pool was situated close to the house in the woods. No more than a couple hundred feet separated the pool from the house.

I was closer to Michael than I thought. Just the thought of going to him, helping him, offered me a trace of hope and a trace was better than nothing at all.

I felt suddenly lighter.

I began to move along the earth floor with increased speed while the sound of rushing water became more intense. A sudden burst of energy filled my veins. But when something stung the back of my leg, I dropped down face-first onto the path like a sack of rags and bones.

My God, had I been shot?

The ground zero of pain was located in the back of my right thigh. From there it rippled throughout my body. The pain shot up and down my backbone with surprising efficiency. I might have rolled over onto my back then, bled to death.

But I attempted to move my feet, then my legs. Pulled myself up from the wet ground, leaned back, felt the welt growing behind my thigh. The wound would've been out of my sight even if it hadn't been dark; I had no way of knowing if a bullet had actually lodged there or merely grazed the skin.

My gut reaction was that I'd just been grazed. Otherwise, I wouldn't be able to move my leg.

Then the whoosh of bullets flying overhead, slapping the foliage. Some of the rounds pinged against the stones and blew up red-yellow sparks. I dropped down hard onto my belly. The bullets came at me fast from behind me, but missing all the time as though Whalen intended for them to miss. And I was sure he did.

Whalen had lived in these woods, hunted them for food. He knew what he was doing. He'd circled around to access the high ground behind me. He no doubt had a night-vision scope to go with his goggles—and a silencer. Some rounds fell short, embedding themselves with a thump into the ground only inches from my face. Water and mud splashed into my eyes, ears, nose, and mouth. The rapid-fire rounds burst through the trees, but not a hint of gunfire or a muzzle flash. The scene was like something out of Michael's manuscripts—guns, bullets, silencers. Not that I was a stranger to firearms. My dad had been a trooper, a hunter, a shooter, a gun collector. I'd lived with guns my entire childhood.

From down on the ground I reached around to my thigh, fingering again the spot of impact. The thick welt had already formed. There was a small tear in the jeans above it. I felt the sting of my touch. Bringing my fingertips back to my face, I raised them to my lips. I tasted the fresh blood.

The rounds kept coming at me fast, furious, and accurately inaccurate. If this weren't like a surreal dream, I would have been too petrified to move. But none of this was real to me. It was all a bizarre dream that only bordered on the real. At least, if I wanted to live, if I wanted Michael to live, that's what I had to believe.

I had to do something. I could either lie there and waste precious time, worry over the pain, worry that I would never wake up from the nightmare, or I could make a move, get myself across the stream and closer to the house in the woods. Closer to Michael. Whalen would have put me down for good if that was what he wanted of me. He clearly had other plans for me. But that didn't mean those plans didn't include clipping me with another shot or two.

A scream pierced the darkness—a yelp coming from behind me along the high ground. The yelp shattered my senses; cut through flesh and bone.

Whalen releasing thirty years of pent-up desire?

I made a silent count to three. With a deep breath, I pushed myself up and onto my feet and bolted off through the brush like an angry field cat.

Chapter 53

I RAN.

The whole of Mount Desolation had become an unrelenting obstacle. Branches whipped and flailed at my face, little devils stinging my arms and chest. I limped and hobbled as fast as I could, off-trail, in a directionless panic, desperate to get myself out of range before one of Whalen's near misses connected again.

My escape should have been a good thing.

But it turned out to be a grave mistake when a head-on collision with a tree trunk knocked me senseless.

Chapter 54

THE NOISE FROM THE SLAMMING DOOR SHOOTS *through me like an ice-cold blade. Even Molly stops her incessant mattress jumping. She stops and stares at me. And me back at her.*

The solid noise of a slamming door…It's a noise you feel as much as hear.

"Must be the wind," Molly says, eyes wide.

"Must be," I agree, although I don't recall much of a breeze blowing outside in those woods.

For what seems forever we just stand still inside the second floor of that home. We wait for another noise to confirm the worst: that we are not alone.

"Maybe it's Dad," Molly whispers.

Trooper Dan.

My stomach caves in on itself. Body grows weak, dizzy. I feel nauseous.

Then a footstep along the first floor. Heavy, leaden. And another.

Footsteps.

"That's not Dad." I swallow, knowing in my heart that it's the boogeyman. The boogeyman who lives in the woods. The boogeyman who killed people. Killed his family.

We wait, paralyzed, not knowing what to do.

The footsteps bear down, growing louder with each step. When I hear the footsteps pounding up the stairs, Molly screams. I drop to my knees.

We're not alone anymore.

Chapter 55

HOW LONG I WAS OUT, I HAVE NO IDEA. A MINUTE, AN hour. Who knows? Lying on my side on the soaked earth I had only a foggy memory of the head-on collision with a tree trunk. All I knew was this: one moment I was trying to run, bullets whizzing by my head, tearing off leaves and twigs, and the next I was opening my eyes to the pain of a tight vice-grip pressure that began and ended in the center of my face. Like two separate sticks that had lodged themselves up inside my nasal passages, the throbbing and stinging tightness made my eyes fill up, my head ring.

I pictured the faces of the people I loved the most. Michael. Molly. Robyn, herself lying in a hospital bed, her face more broken than my own, a little baby growing inside of her. I wondered if I would ever see her again. I wondered if I would live long enough to see her child.

Lifting my right hand, I extended the index finger, gently touching the bridge of my nose. I felt the surface sting where the cartilage had fractured, the skin split down the middle. I could breathe, but only through my mouth.

My nose was broken.

Blood combined with the rain, running thick onto my lips and tongue. It tasted of salt and water. There was a sick, inside-out sensation in my stomach. I heard another shriek coming through the trees, not far behind me. Whalen knew these woods like he must have known his own face. His thirty-year absence from them would make no difference. He must have re-created them a thousand times before in the solitary confines of his prison cell. I heard the rustling of leaves and branches. Still, I could not see him. His presence was invisible to me. He was a short but stocky man. He hadn't grown old in prison like Detective Harris had said. The monster had only grown stronger. More violent. More determined. The noise sounded like a bear crashing through the forest.

That's when I felt them on my legs.

The snakes.

Maybe I couldn't see, hear, or smell them, but I could feel their thick, rubbery, legless bodies slithering over my lower legs, one after the other as if I were laid out atop a nest.

The garden snakes frightened me almost as much as Whalen. All that rain must have forced them out of their holes, out from their havens in between the rocks. They were crawling on me and I could not move. I was immobile, catatonic.

I had to move. I had to get out of there, get away from the devil, away from the snakes. Inhaling, I issued a nearly silent shriek and forced myself up.

Several snakes fell to the ground. In the dark I couldn't be sure how many. But I felt and heard the sound of their rubbery bodies coiling against the leaves and the pine needles. With the powerless flashlight gripped in my right hand, I shuffled through the thick woods. Not in any specific direction, but away from the snakes, away from the boogeyman crashing through the trees.

Without warning, I fell.

Chapter 56

THE WHIRLING CURRENT TOOK HOLD OF MY BODY, drawing me into its center. I felt myself being pulled under, body spiraling, going down. I had no choice but to let myself go, be drawn under the surface of the drowning pool, be dragged along the rocky bottom of a rushing stream, spit out over the waterfall.

I didn't free fall to the rocky streambed below. I reached out, clawing for something to grab onto, my nails bending back and tearing. Until I found a handhold in the form of a thick tree root that protruded from the cliffside, and hung there, legs dangling.

Flash of lightning—multiple, spider-veined strikes to my right, ripped through the curtain of water that spewed over the cliff edge enough to show the flash-lit valley downstream in its gaps. The rushing stream water shot downward through the black night to pummel the invisible rocks below, some of it falling onto me as I swayed into its path from where I dangled by the tree root.

Hugging the rock face, I searched for a foothold against the loose shale until I managed to locate solid footing. Gripping tightly, I pulled and chinned myself up and over the tree root. When my head was above the rock-face's edge, I raised my right leg and located a secure toehold.

Pressing my full weight down on the right foot, I let go of the tree root and thrust my right hand over the cliff edge. I then pushed my palm down flat onto the wet, gravelly floor. With my left hand still secured to the root, all I needed was to lift my body up and over the side.

It's precisely what I started to do when my right hand exploded in pain.

Chapter 57

I FACED MY NIGHTMARE IN THE FLESH. WHALEN STOOD over me, green goggles covering his eyes, masking his face. He stood erect, body dripping rainwater. I sensed him with every nerve and neuron in my body.

His right foot had come down on my right hand, boot heel crushing flesh and bone. The pain shot through my arm, past my elbow, into my shoulder, then up into my head. The entire right side of my body was on fire. I screamed, my voice howling into a night punctuated with rain, thunder, and darkness. I heard my own voice echoing off the cliffside, shooting out into the valley, out over the deep woods, out over the fields of tall grass, out over the valley and the farmlands.

I felt the pain with every exposed nerve in my body. I held to the edge, ran my free hand over the shale wall, searched for a chunk of loose rock until I felt one about the size of my own hand. The rock was smooth on one side, with a sharp, jagged edge on the other. I fit the rock into the palm of my left hand, gripped it with every ounce of my strength. Then, with one swift downward swing of my arm, thrust the sharp edge into his foot.

He screamed, his high-pitched voice crying out into the deep night. He was now the suddenly maimed monster. Whalen may have had the power to see in the night, but he hadn't anticipated the chunk of sharp shale coming for his foot. He yanked his right foot out from under the tip of the sharpened edge and fell flat onto his back.

The pain left me then.

There was only the bleeding and a rush of energy that shot up from the tips of my toes, entering into my limbs. I did not pull myself over the edge so much as leap over it, landing directly on top of him.

I wasn't me anymore. I'd become my sister.

It was as if Molly—her strength, her fearlessness, her courage—had entered into my body and my soul. Pressing knees against Whalen's arms, I managed to pick up another rock about the size of my palm. I raised it high and swung it down like a mallet. There was the good feel of a tooth or maybe teeth breaking on contact, his lips popping, gums tearing. Two narrow, incandescent eyes stared up at me while the monster once more screamed a high-pitched yodel that cut not only through the forest, but sliced its way into my skull and brain.

I loved every second of it. *Molly* loved every second. We'd been waiting for a chance like this for thirty years. Not even death was going to keep Mol from having her revenge.

I swung the rock wildly, hitting the monster again and again. But the pain I inflicted seemed to do no good. Whalen lifted his head, spit blood into my face, and smiled. The boogeyman smiled, worked up a gurgled laugh while swinging his right arm around so quickly, I never saw the rock that slammed against my skull.

Now it was me who was on my back, left side of my head pounding in rapid stinging pulses.

I glared up at green eyes. "Kill me *now*! Do it now, fucker!"

The air went abruptly still. The thunder and lightning, the rain, the wind all seemed to halt their fury as if God Himself were creating a still life of the scene. Whalen wiped his mouth with the back of his gloved hand, did it without the least bit of effort, as though impervious to the pain.

He spit another wad of blood and spittle.

"Little...kitten...has...lost...her...mittens," he whispered through clenched, broken, blood-stained teeth. "Cry, cry, cry, little kitten."

From down on my back I stared up into the mechanical green eyes, at the rainwater that dribbled down off his shaved head, down onto bloody lips. I tried to speak. But no words would come. Only the silent motion of a mouth opening and closing. As if responding to the silence, he reared back and away from me.

Just like that, the boogeyman shot off into the night.

Chapter 58

DOWN FLAT ON MY BACK, I SUCKED WET AIR THROUGH a gaping mouth. I opened my eyes, rolled over, and pushed myself up onto my feet. I had crossed the stream and nearly gotten myself killed in the process. But it was something I had to do if I was to stay on Michael's trail. Stuffing my damaged hand into my jeans, I turned my back on the stream and approached the tree line.

Bushwhacking almost blindly through thick greenbrier and second growth saplings, the sound of stream water grew more prominent with each step forward. I had no choice but to swallow the pain, ignore the five senses and focus instead on the anger, on the determination to reach Michael.

But there was something I had to do before anything else. My nose was broken. I couldn't leave it like that. If I was going to get to Michael, I needed to breathe through it. Without thinking, I cupped the broken nose inside my two hands. Supporting the fleshy nostril portion between opposing thumbs, I sucked a deep breath through my mouth, cracked the cartilage back in place.

I released a strained shriek that shot off into the valley.

But when the sting went away, I sensed only a dull soreness where the skin was split.

There was one more thing I had to do. It dawned on me that maybe if I opened up the flashlight, shifted the batteries around, there'd be enough power left in them to give me light. Even if only for the few minutes it took to get to the house. That's exactly what my father used to do when I was little and the power went out. He'd make the flashlight batteries last longer by shifting them around inside the tube. I pulled the flashlight from my pant waist, unscrewed the end, poured the batteries out into my hand, reversed their original order, and reloaded them into the tube. Holding my breath, I switched the light on.

It worked. I had light. Not a strong light, but enough of a dull yellow glow for me to see my way through the darkness.

With the dull light to guide me, I took off.

Trekking through the thick growth, the rain poured down even harder than before. It came down with such force, it penetrated the tree cover, raindrops shooting and scooting between the now illuminated leaves like a spray of bright-yellow paint. The rain smacked against my face, stinging the laceration on my nose. For the first time since having been dropped into the woods, I felt like I had to come to grips with my exhaustion.

I was dead tired. Tired *and* wired. I was living a very bad dream and all was as surreal as it was the real deal. Branches slapped and jabbed at my face. It was as if the trees had eyes and saw me coming. But I didn't feel the pain and sting anymore. I felt only the urgent need to get to Michael.

I knew then that Whalen was going to kill us. That it was only a matter of time. I didn't want to die alone. Not at the hands of the devil. I wanted to die alongside Michael, wanted to die in his arms, the two of us married once more.

Chapter 59

HE'S A SHORT MAN. STOCKY AND STRONG. HE'S DRESSED in filthy khakis, work boots, a white T-shirt that's turned filthy gray, and a green baseball hat with the words "Christian Brothers Academy" sewn across its front above the brim. His face is gaunt and covered in black stubble. He's holding a pistol. He doesn't say a word when he grabs hold of my hair and pulls me in toward him.

When Molly comes at him, her hands and fingers held before her like claws, he cocks back that pistol, hits her over the head with the butt. She falls like a rock beside me on the floor.

I want to scream, but the pain in my head is too great. The boogeyman grabs hold of my hair with one hand and tries to caress it with the other. It's the first time a man other than my father has touched my hair and I become immediately nauseous.

I feel him shiver, his body quake.

"Two little kittens," he chants. "Two little kittens have lost their mittens and they begin to cry. You naughty kittens. Now you shall have no pie."

"I'm sorry," I plead, tears streaming down my face. "I'm sorry, sorry, sorry."

"And they begin to cry," he repeats. "Cry, cry, cry."

He drags me downstairs and leaves me on the warped living room floor not far from the front door. Then he goes back up after

Molly. I want to get up and run out the door but I'm afraid he'll kill her. The door is right there, I can almost touch it. All I have to do is get up and open it and run. But I can't leave Molly. Can't leave my twin sister.

Molly is coming to by the time she is laid out on the floor beside me. Without a word about his intentions, Whalen is kneeling over us. He's tearing off these extra long pieces of duct tape, wrapping them around my right wrist and Molly's left wrist so that we're joined together. When he's finished, he yanks us up onto our feet.

"Little kittens have lost their mittens," he chants, "Run away, little kittens, so I can catch you. Cry, cry, cry."

Molly is more awake now. But she's not saying anything.

The man presses his forearm against his eyes. "I'm counting, little kittens," he sings.

"Run," Molly insists. "Any way we can, as fast we can."

Chapter 60

I BROKE THROUGH THE TREE LINE, THE FLASHLIGHT'S trembling beam lighting the way. I spotted the stream where it curved back around again and once more cut off my direct path to Michael. I scanned the beam of dull flashlight over the surface of the stream, searched for a way to get across without being dragged under by the storm-fed white water. I looked for that old bridge of boulders that Molly and I had used—the one with one rock succeeding another. I looked for a lightning-struck tree that might have fallen across the stream's width. With only the dull illumination from the flashlight and not a hint of star or moonlight, I found neither.

My hand was broken, my ribs stinging, and my face split down the center. If I tried to swim, I'd drown. I moved my way upstream for maybe thirty feet, then downstream until I came to the edge of the pool.

No way across the open water. No way across. No rocks, no felled tree, no shallow land bridge. The house in the woods was located on the opposite side of the winding stream. Michael was held hostage in the basement of that house.

I made my way back upstream and stood on the edge of the bank, feeling the oily mist on my face from the stream's white force. I had to think like Molly. *What would Molly do if she were in my boots?* I knew exactly what she would do. Once more I stuffed the flashlight into my jeans, teetered on the edge of the white water, and gulped down my dread.

I jumped.

Chapter 61

WE SKIP AND HOP OUR WAY DOWN THE PORCH STAIRS,
onto a narrow path that leads out into the woods. Molly has regained
some of her strength. Groggily, she pulls me along.

"Come on," she says in a muted but intense voice. "We can make
it out of here if we try."

But I'm slowing her down. I'm so scared I can hardly move.
We're identical Siamese twins, joined at the wrists. I'm crying, trip-
ping, struggling to keep up.

Together we fall along the path.

Molly screams, "Get up! Get up!"

I cry, try to lift myself, but we fall again. I try again to raise
myself up and this time it works. We raise ourselves up together. We
hobble along the path until we hear the sound of the stream.

"All we have to do is get across that stream," she exclaims. "Then
we cross it again farther downhill, and then we try for home."

We keep moving, playing the man's awful game of cat and
mouse. All the while the sound of rushing stream water gets louder,
more forceful. When we come to its edge, Molly asks me if I'm ready.
Ready to jump in, that is.

She would pull me in if isn't for the gunshot.

Chapter 62

THE ICE-COLD WHITE WATER DRAGGED ME DOWN-stream. I held out my hands for anything I could latch onto. Body twisting and turning in the water, I grabbed onto a rock with both hands and arms. For maybe a second or two I managed to stop my downstream progress toward the pool. But it didn't take long for the smooth, moss-covered rock to betray me. As the frigid water pulled at my body and the rock slipped out of my hands, I felt my body once more being carried away.

My head and body were pulled underneath the water's surface. I swallowed water; I was drowning. Until my head would once more reemerge, only to be sucked under again. Deeper this time, the water filling my lungs, choking me.

But instead of panic, an explosion of anger erupted inside of me. It built up and up until nothing mattered anymore. Not my pain, not the cold, not exhaustion, not the suffocating sensation of drowning. Not fear. There was only the need to beat the stream, to beat my fear, to put an end to Whalen. To get to Michael.

The pull of the rushing water yanked me under, pulled me downstream. I held my breath and clawed at the stream bank for something to grab onto. When my body slammed into a felled tree that had been completely submerged by heavy water, I felt a burning pain in my ribcage as I swallowed stream water. Using my good hand, I grabbed hold of one of the branches and grasped it as tightly as I could. It worked. Pulling myself up from the stream, I spit out the water that filled my mouth and lungs. Then I sucked in a deep breath of sweet oxygen. I planted my right foot in the secure place of the tree where the branch met its thick trunk. With my last breath, I heaved my torso up and over the stream bank.

Chapter 63

I STOOD FROZEN, WATER-SOAKED, BRUISED, AND afraid. But I was also proud of myself. Strong. It must have been the way Molly felt so many times in her life. I swore I had to be smiling. I could feel the muscles in my jaws constricting, tightening. A smile, despite everything that had happened to me in the woods.

My drenched body shivered.

I shined the light upstream. Through the trees and the thick brush, I could make out the clapboard farmhouse. The flashlight's dull beam lit up the exterior wall. Just ahead of me was a narrow trail. I burst into an all-out sprint along that trail in the direction of the house.

Body tingled, head buzzed, lungs filled with oxygen. My feet moved rapidly beneath me, the pain in my legs having all but disappeared. Not ten feet of trail separated me from the house in the woods when a hand reached out, grabbing hold of my long blonde hair.

Chapter 64

HE'S RIGHT BEHIND US. THE BOOGEYMAN IS FOLLOWING
us the entire time. He grabs Molly's hair, pulls it back.

She screams. He laughs.

"Cry, cry, cry," he spits.

He pulls mine. I begin to weep. I fall, bringing Molly down
with me.

There's a pistol barrel in our faces. Then he is tucking the pistol
into his pant waist. Bending, he grabs my left foot and Molly's right,
starts dragging us back across the narrow foot trail to the house.

"Little kittens lost their mittens. Cry, cry, cry, little kittens."

When he gets us to the porch, he pulls out a long silver knife
from the sheath on his belt, cuts the tape that binds our wrists. I lie
still on the ground while Molly tries to run. But he is too quick for
her. He grabs hold of her T-shirt, drags her back down, and once
more whips her over the head with the pistol grip.

Molly goes to sleep again.

That's when the devil grabs hold of me. The devil drags me up
the porch steps, through the open front door, across the floor, through
a door that leads to a black, rank basement.

He pulls me down the basement stairs by my hair. My spine
pounds against the wooden treads. At the bottom of the stairs he
pulls me across the cold dirt floor. He handcuffs me to something. It's

pitch dark. The place smells of must, urine, and death. I'm shivering with fear and disbelief.

An overhead light comes on.

I can see that I'm chained to this iron pipe in the middle of a square room. It's constructed of stone and concrete, narrow casement windows located at the very top of the walls. Big metal hooks have been bolted into the bottoms of the exposed rafters. They look like the hooks the farmers use to hang their freshly butchered meat. From where I sit, I can see that the hooks are stained with blood.

For a time, the man just stares down at me. He's breathing hard.

"What are you going to do to me?" I beg, the handcuffs tight and cutting into my wrists.

"Cry, cry, cry, little kitten," he sings.

I scream.

But only the boogeyman can hear me.

Chapter 65

WHALEN LET GO OF MY HAIR AND PRESSED THE PISTOL barrel against the small of my back.

"Walk, little kitten. Walk."

I did it, walked toward the house without a word of protest. As we approached I began to make out the low hum of an engine running. I knew the only explanation for it had to be a generator. Whalen must have been feeding power to the relic of a rotting house. For what reason, I had no idea. No doubt I would find out soon.

I wasn't frightened anymore. I felt resolved, somehow. I knew what was coming, where I was going. I'd known for a while now where I was going. I'd been there before. In a strange way I *wanted* to go back down there. The situation reeked of inevitability, as if I'd been waiting for this moment for thirty years, as if what happened to Molly and me when we were twelve was merely a prologue to this very moment in time. I wanted to go back down there if only to be with Michael, to finish this thing while holding him tightly.

We entered the house.

Whalen used his own flashlight to light the way across a floor that over three decades had warped and rotted. When we came to the door that led into the basement, I could see that an electric light was already on. Now I knew the reason for the generator.

When he gave me a shove, I resisted. But when he pushed me again, I lost my footing and fell.

I slid down the wooden stairs, my body slamming against each tread. By the time I landed, I thought I'd pass out from the pain. My vision distorted, going in and out of focus.

He descended the stairs, the soles of his leather boots stamping the treads one by one. I could already smell him. When he made it to the bottom, he tucked his pistol into the waist of his filthy dungarees, slipped his hands under my arms, and dragged me across the dirt floor. My head hung so that I was staring up at the exposed beams, at the meat hooks that descended from them.

He reached down and touched my lips with his fingers. When I bit his hand, I tasted blood.

He reared back with his hand, slapped my face.

As he straightened up, I laid my head back. The figure caught my eye. The figure of a man. Arms, legs, and torso hanging upside down from the ceiling. Bare feet chained to the rafters.

Michael.

Whalen had hung him upside down like a slaughtered animal. My eyes filled with the sight of his lifeless body. I screamed without making a sound. I sobbed without shedding a tear. I died, though my heart beat on.

Chapter 66

I AM NEARLY DELIRIOUS WITH FEAR BY THE TIME HE drags Molly down into the basement and lays her out beside me. I can see that she's awake, her eyes going from me to him to me again. He looks at her with a calm, confident smile.

I sense that Molly is about to scream, cry.

But she doesn't. She grits her teeth, stares the devil in the eye and spits in his face.

He slaps her.

She glares back at him, as if working up the courage to do it again. But she doesn't spit in his face. Instead she does something entirely different. She inhales a deep breath. Settles back. Goes limp. "Don't struggle against him, Bec," she insists. "Promise me you won't struggle."

I look away.

Chapter 67

I CAME TO.

How long had I been passed out?

Long enough for him to dig a good-sized trench in the dirt floor. For a time I just locked my eyes onto him, watched him working, a lit cigarette dangling from his lips. That wiry body soaked with sweat, plastered with dirt and filth, reeking of tobacco. Tiny, yellow teeth ground against one another while he worked, shoveling one spade full of dirt at a time.

Then he caught sight of me. He saw that I was conscious and he smiled.

"Hello, little kitten," he said, softly. "Cry, cry, cry, little kitten."

I knew then that what he had in store had nothing to do with his old motivation—his taste for young girls. There would be no touching here. No violations.

There would only be death.

He reached for me. I had no strength left in me to resist. He dragged me the few feet to the trench. He dumped me in. I did a complete roll, landing on my back. I heard him laugh. At least, I thought it was a laugh. It might just as easily have been a sob. He was standing above me, the little monster of a boogeyman looking almost huge now. Godlike.

He had that shovel in his hand.

He stabbed at the dirt pile, retrieved a shovelful of earth, held it over my prone body, and tossed it into the trench. The dirt smacked my body, sprayed into my face. It invaded my mouth, nostrils; I shook my head to keep it from blocking my air supply.

There was something inside the dirt. Something other than rock and gravel and clay. Black-and-white-colored shards of bone covered me. A jaw bone, the teeth still embedded in the broken jaw. A small portion of skullcap. A leg bone. Were these the remains of the victims of Whalen's torture?

Another shovelful of bone-filled dirt fell onto me, this one down by my feet.

He was burying me alive.

Yet another shovel of dirt slapped my face. I coughed, then choked as a worm wiggled in my mouth. Spitting it out, I tried to wipe the dirt from my eyes, but all my strength bled out. I was already dead. I could still see him, but only through a cloud of dirt and pain.

The bone shards and dirt kept coming, filling the trench, filling my mouth and nostrils. With each shovelful, another bit of life emptied out of me.

I was still alive, but already dead.

Chapter 68

MOLLY DOESN'T RESIST.

I don't resist when he unlocks me from the radiator, grabs my hair.

No struggling.

How did Molly know? Our passivity seems to make the monster sad. He has Molly on the dirt floor on her back. He's pinning her shoulders against the floor. She does nothing to resist.

He can't go through with it. He can't do it. He grabs hold of me.

I don't resist.

He throws me on my back.

I don't resist.

His lips form a pout. He stands up and begins to cry.

"Cry, cry, cry," he chants through his own tears.

As though ashamed of his tears, he turns away from us, hides his face with his arm. Molly and I turn to one another, lie on the dirt floor hugging one another. Until Molly spots something. Only a few feet away, a shovel. She lets go of me, lunges for the shovel, and stands with it gripped in her hand. He's sobbing, still bent over. She slowly stands, raises the shovel high, brings it down hard on the boogeyman's head.

He drops face-first to the dirt.

Molly drops the shovel, falls to her knees next to me on the dirty floor, and takes me in her arms. We shiver, we cry, and we hold one another.

We did not resist.

We did not resist.

We did not resist.

Molly gets back up onto her feet. She wipes her eyes, stemming a silent flow of tears. A streak of brown mud marks the right side of her face.

"That's enough, Bec," she says, with a stone face.

With that, she reaches her hand out for me, helping me up off the dirt floor.

Chapter 69

THEN I SPOTTED SOMEBODY ELSE. A SHORT, SQUAT silhouette of a man.

I stared at the man through the dirt and tears. Only I was aware of him.

Franny.

It was Franny and he had something in his hand. An iron bar of some kind. A two- or three-foot length of rusted rebar.

Franny.

Franny was holding the iron bar two-fisted over Whalen's head. Unaware of Franny's presence, Whalen went about his work filling in the trench, burying me. It was all happening now in slow motion, one frame slowly following another as that iron bar came down, smacking Whalen in the center of his skull. Even from deep down inside the trench, the sound of metal coming down against skull and brain was like a mallet smacked against a rotting pumpkin. A sickening blow. His black eyes went wide as his knees gave out, and he collapsed onto my dirt-covered stomach.

Franny dropped the iron bar to the floor.

He came to me, bent down, and rolled Whalen off me. He extended his left hand.

"Safe. Safe, safe, safe."

Chapter 70

WITH FRANNY'S HELP, I MANAGED TO GET BACK UP onto my feet. As the fresh dirt fell off me, I stood wobbly and spit out tiny bits of skeletal remains of the long departed. I tried to spit out the taste of death.

But it was impossible.

Even to Franny I must have appeared a strange, desperate sight with my filthy clothing, cuts and bruises, and matted hair. Outside the house now you could hear the sound of thunder. Franny tried to brush off some of the dirt from my arms and face.

I grabbed hold of his hand and kissed it. I knew how much he hated to be touched by another human being, but he didn't resist. I felt my lips on his hand. I smelled his skin, listened to his breaths. He averted his eyes and stared at the dirt floor.

Not three feet away, Whalen's body occupied a trench meant for me. An open grave. His head was bleeding. Not a muscle in his body moved. The monster was finally dead.

Cry, cry, cry…

But what if he wasn't dead? What if he was alive still?

Behind me, Michael's body hung upside down from the ceiling, a blood pool directly below him staining the dirt floor, soaking it.

I wanted to go to him. Franny somehow knew this. "No, Rebecca. NO! NO! NO!"

He put his arm around me, lifting me up off my feet. As I burst into tears, he carried me across the floor, up the stairs, out of the house, and into the woods.

Chapter 71

A GRAY DAWN ERUPTED OVER MOUNT DESOLATION AS we tore through the forest. We took no chances. By the time we made it to the stream bank, we hit the water running. The frigid white water was a shock to my body.

But I didn't scream.

Franny held onto me, wrapped his arms around me, keeping both our heads and shoulders just barely above water, feet kicking beneath him against the current.

As I held onto him with all the strength I had left in me, Franny pumped and pumped. But the storm-driven white water was too powerful, too relentless. I didn't care. I wanted to drown. Still I held on, my arms wrapped around his shoulders and neck, fingernails digging into his skin.

The current dragged us under. But I didn't panic, even when I swallowed water into my lungs. The water pulled us down. It poured over our heads. It filled our mouths. Until suddenly we reemerged gasping for breath, water flowing out of our nostrils and mouths like blood from stab wounds.

I knew that if the stream were any wider, it would have consumed us entirely.

But the stream was not wide. Despite its pull, momentum was on our side. As the opposite bank approached, we swam and kicked. The cold water injected new life into our veins. It washed away the blood and the dirt that came from the devil's basement.

When Franny reached out with his free hand and grasped a handhold along the opposite bank, I knew for sure we would survive. Pulling me in toward him, he wrenched my forearm off his neck. At the same time, I felt a thick tree root sticking out of the bank. I gripped the root with both hands while my legs and feet continued downstream, the current twisting my body sideways, parallel with the bank.

Now side by side in the stream, holding onto the bank, I somehow managed a breath. With drenched bodies and faces, we gazed at one another for the briefest of moments before thrusting our bodies up and out of the streaming water onto the safety of the solid earth.

Chapter 72

WE EMERGE FROM THE HOUSE IN THE WOODS ARM IN arm.

I'm still crying. But Molly is not. I know she's convinced that the boogeyman is dead. Even I believe he's dead.

Molly is a rock.

She shushes me, tells me it's going to be OK. She leads me through the woods, to the sound of water running brusquely over rocks.

When we come to the stream bank, she sets me down. She cups her right hand, reaches into the stream, and brings a handful of the water to my mouth.

"Drink," she says.

I do as she tells me.

The crystal-clear water is cold, life-renewing. It tastes pure, sweet.

In my mind I see him, what he tried to do to us. I'm sure he's dead, but I'm frightened he'll come back for us. I say nothing about it. So long as Molly is with me, I can bear anything.

"Don't worry," she insists. "The monster is dead now."

She tells me to lie back. She dips her hand in the water once more, then brings the wet hand to my face. I can smell her hands. She runs her fingers through my hair, over my eyes and lips. She washes my neck and arms. She touches me softly, bathes my body and my legs.

Finally, she washes my feet with the cold stream water. When she is done, she sets her own feet into the stream and washes her own body. I watch her wash her hair with the water until it is dripping wet.

When we are washed, we sit on the bank in silence, allowing ourselves to dry in the cool air. Although we are shivering from the cold, we don't feel it. We feel only the recent memory of that afternoon. We feel a pain like we have never felt before and hope never to again. We never talk about saying anything to our parents about the attacks. It's already implied that we'll remain silent about exploring the dark woods our father forbade us to enter.

As the sun begins to set, Molly takes my hand and leads me to the place in the rocky stream where we can easily cross.

She kisses me on the forehead.

"I am you," she says. "And you are me."

Together, we head for home through the trees.

Chapter 73

FOR A TIME THAT SEEMED FOREVER, WE RAN DOWNHILL toward the fields of tall grass. There was no talking. Not that Franny would have said anything anyway. There was simply no breath left in our lungs. In my lungs, anyway.

On the outside was the vision of the fields and my parents' house looking small and isolated in the distance. On the inside my heart beat, pulse soared, blood pumped through wiry veins while the misty cool air of a new morning burned up lung tissue.

We didn't head for my parents' house. Instead I followed Franny through the fields, limping up a gentle incline until eventually I spotted the Scaramuzzi farm. By this time, the day was warming and I was having trouble breathing and keeping my balance. Then, as though a car crashed into me, my chest constricted, the center cramped in tight pain, a shooting jolt of lightning in my left arm.

When I collapsed, Franny came to me and lifted me up in his arms. He carried me like that the rest of the way.

When we finally made it to his house, he set me gently down onto the porch.

Although I couldn't see her, I heard Caroline Scaramuzzi gasp. She wasted no time dialing 9-1-1. I fell in and out of consciousness as she spoke with the emergency people, as I mumbled, "Michael... inside house...in woods...Michael."

I wasn't scared. I was no longer in pain. I was caught up in a semiconscious state I'd never before experienced. I wondered if I was dying. Dying wasn't so bad. Dying meant that I would see Molly before the day was out.

Before long, I was flying.

Chapter 74

A HELICOPTER WAS CALLED IN TO TRANSPORT ME FROM Brunswick Hills to the Albany Medical Center. After being lifted off the porch floor of the Scaramuzzi house, I found myself floating far above the valley. I was lying on my back, a translucent oxygen mask covering my face. When I turned my head I could see the deep blue-green water of the Hudson River snaking north to south between the cities of Troy and Albany. There was the loud *whump-whump-whump* of the chopper blades—a sound I felt deep inside my chest.

I looked for Michael, as if everything that had transpired over the past dozen hours was an elaborate nightmare. But instead I found Caroline Scaramuzzi. She was strapped into a seat that folded out of the aircraft's sidewall. From where I lay belted to a collapsible gurney, I could see that she was dressed in her usual blue jeans, thick fisherman's sweater, and green Crocs.

I felt Michael's absence like a hole in my belly.

I locked eyes with Caroline. I allowed her image to guide me back to the land of the unconscious.

Chapter 75

ANOTHER DAY PASSED BEFORE I WOKE UP. LYING IN THE hospital bed, I had no other choice but to believe the truth: I was alive.

How did I know this?

First off, my head ached. My temples pounded. I felt empty on the inside. Nauseous and so very thirsty. I tasted only my own bitter breath. I smelled the vague odor of alcohol in the air. All was quiet.

A glance over my shoulder did not reveal Franny, nor Caroline, for that matter. Rather, it revealed Detective Harris. The tall, suited man smoothed out his cropped hair, gazed into my newly opened eyes. Maybe it was my imagination, but I swear he was trying to work up a welcome smile when he said, "You've been through quite an ordeal."

A smile. For certain he was smiling.

Attempting to shift my shell-shocked body up against the head-board, I wrenched and strained to no avail. Movement proved an impossible dream. Any kind of movement, no matter how slight, caused a sharp pain to pulse up and down my spinal column. It also caused the heart monitor to which I was attached to pick up speed.

"Michael?" I whispered.

Harris crossed his arms.

"Michael is still recovering from surgery," he said, looking away. "He's lost a lot of blood, Rebecca."

I tried to move, but I couldn't.

"Michael's alive? But how…"

I needed to see Michael. I needed to know that I wasn't dreaming.

"You can see him soon," he explained. "But Rebecca, I need you to talk to me. I need you to tell me everything."

I lay back, stared up at the ceiling, breathed.

After a time, I led him through the whole ordeal. From the time Michael and I returned to my apartment on Thursday afternoon, to Franny's rescue of me inside the basement of the house in the woods.

When I was done, Harris just sat there for a time, chewing on the information. Clearly something wasn't sitting right with the detective. He stood up, turned his back, and stared out the window onto the parking lot below.

"By the time my men got to the house in the woods," he said, "by the time we got to Michael—Whalen was gone, vanished."

I felt my insides tighten up. I wondered if the monitor would pick up the change.

"We followed a blood trail out of the house and into the woods. But after a while it disappeared, along with our suspect." He shook his head, eyes peeled out the window. But when he turned back to me, he tried to plant that same smile on his face. A reassuring smile that screamed *lie*.

"I don't want you to worry," he assured me. "If his head injury is as bad as you painted it, there's a good chance that his body will be found in those woods as early as this morning or this afternoon."

How had Whalen had been able to leave the halfway house without being detected? How had he been able to follow me for all those weeks and months? How had he been able to kidnap Michael and me if he was supposed to be reporting to a job or a halfway house?

I shot the questions to Harris. Angrily, bitterly, as if he were personally responsible.

In turn he shrugged his shoulders, bit his lip. "Halfway houses are not prisons, Rebecca," he offered. "Parole officers are not ball-and-chains. Ankle monitors can be hacked and removed, if you know what you're doing. The system of keeping a twenty-four-hour watch on a parolee, even a violent offender like Whalen, is not perfect. All it would take for him to get some extra time outside the house is a little money and maybe the confidence of one or more of his counselors. That's about it, I'm afraid."

He put his hand on my hand, squeezing my fingers. He told me not to think about Whalen anymore.

I looked up at him, into his eyes. "Thirty years ago," I said, "when Whalen dragged us into the basement. He never actually…" I hesitated, because I didn't know how to say it.

"He never actually what?"

"When he had Molly on the floor, she turned to me, told me not to resist. She made me promise not to resist. When she allowed Whalen to do what he wanted, he no longer wanted to do it. He couldn't go through with it with either of us, because we wouldn't resist him."

The detective nodded. His hand was still holding mine.

"But he still violated you," he said. "He hurt you and he hurt your sister. He abducted you and held you against your will."

I wasn't sure how to feel about my confession; how to feel about the possibility of Whalen still being alive.

"Get some rest," Harris said, releasing my hand. "You're going to need it."

I closed my eyes. It felt good to close my eyes. Already I felt myself nodding off.

"Dead," I mumbled in my near sleep state. "Find...the devil... dead."

Chapter 76

BY THE TIME I OPENED MY EYES AGAIN, IT WAS GOING on late morning. A nurse stood beside the bed holding my left hand in her hand, the pads of her middle and index fingers pressed against my wrist. When she was through, she jotted some information onto a clipboard.

She then tossed a smile for the brokenhearted to the woman whose leg had been grazed by a bullet, who'd suffered a mild heart attack, plus two broken ribs, a hairline fracture in her right hand, numerous abrasions, contusions, and lacerations.

The nurse shifted her eyes toward the door. "Looks like we have some visitors," she said before slipping out the door.

Enter Caroline and Franny.

Franny, my hero.

Caroline, dressed in her jeans and Crocs; Franny, dressed in his baggy jeans, red T-shirt, bright-yellow suspenders, thick gray-black hair all mussed up.

"Come here, Franny," I whispered, my voice forcing itself out of my dry mouth and burning throat.

There was something in his hands. Another canvas. It dawned on me then: there had to be a fifth painting. That is, if he were to complete the project he'd assigned himself. Five senses required a fifth and final painting. He set it against the chair, its image facing the opposite direction. He came to me, stood up against the side of the bed, face down, eyes staring down at his shoes.

"Can I hug you?" I asked him.

Out the corner of my eyes, I saw Caroline smiling. "Go ahead, Franny," she pressed. "It'll be OK."

Without lifting his eyes, he leaned into me. I took hold of him. Although I had very little strength left in my arms, I hugged him as tightly as possible. He held himself rigid in my embrace, but he did not pull away.

"Thank you, Franny," I whispered into his ear. "I love you."

I felt a tear run down my cheek. I felt my face touching his. I knew he could feel the tear against his skin too.

"You're my friend," he mumbled.

I let him go. He stood up, went back over to the corner, where he stood by the painting, as if guarding it.

Caroline turned to him. "Fran," she said, reaching into her jeans pocket, producing a five-dollar bill. "Go down to the cafeteria. Get a hot chocolate and a piece of pie. You can enjoy it right there. When you're done come back up here."

Without a single word of objection, Franny took the money and, mumbling something happy about pie and hot chocolate, exited the room.

Caroline turned to me then. With pursed lips, she approached me. She had something in her hand. A paperback book. My old dog-eared copy of *To Kill a Mockingbird*. She set it on the bed beside me.

"I thought you might want this," she said.

Then, pulling one of the chairs closer to the bed, she sat down and exhaled. She asked me how I was feeling, if I needed anything. She told me she would take me down to see Michael as soon as he was out of recovery. She would do it even if she had to strap me onto her shoulders. Then she told me not to worry about anything. That if money was an issue, she would take care of it. She told me not even to think of arguing with her.

I didn't.

Then she began to tell me a story about the past. Not my past, but her past, my father's and mother's past. It was about an event that took place in the early 1960s before I was born. Back when my father had just begun his career as a state trooper for Rensselaer County, back when the house in the woods was not a house in the woods at all, but a house surrounded by farmland.

"There had always been something terrible surrounding that home," she said. "It was a dark place, the house not kept up, the vegetation that surrounded it overgrown and neglected. They had a few animals, but pathetic stock. Your father had just moved to his place at the time and had, in fact, purchased his spread from the Whalens. They were always desperate for money so eventually they sold off most of what they owned, including a good-sized parcel of Mount Desolation."

She looked away from me, toward the window.

"The Whalen family was what you might refer to in today's day and age as dysfunctional. The father was a heavy drinker—an alcoholic. Rarely did he emerge from the house, other than to start up his truck, drive it into town for groceries and of course, whiskey. Mrs. Whalen did the best she could raising a daughter and a son on what little money came in. Although it was never proven, it was widely believed that young Joseph took the brunt of his father's anger.

"I believe his father beat him, beat him terribly. Joseph was an abused boy and like many abused boys he grew up to be cruel. He was eventually dismissed from high school for stalking and then inappropriately touching a girl in his class. The incident was kept hush-hush. Not a strange thing for the day. But Joseph was asked not to come back and I think for him it was a relief. He spent his days and nights on the farm after that, rarely leaving it, hunting and fishing for food, growing what he could.

"Things were quiet for some time, until one night not long before President Kennedy was assassinated, we all awoke to a fire. The Whalens' barn was burning. The fire lit up the night sky and we all came out of our houses to see it. My husband and I got in the truck and drove down to your parents' place. Your father and mother were already up and holding vigil outside in the driveway. She was pregnant at the time with a baby that eventually miscarried. Your father had this look on his face I remember. It was a cross between worried and downright furious. The door to the squad car assigned to him was open and the radio was spitting out orders. Your dad was being ordered to investigate the scene while fire and police backup were on their way.

"What he found inside that house that night shook up our small community something terrible. Joseph shot them all while they lay asleep in their beds. His mother, father, and sister. Your father found them like that, in their beds. He found Joseph sitting outside the barn, the shotgun in his hands, just staring unblinking at the fire."

Caroline's story might have sounded new and shocking enough to raise the tiny hairs up on the back of my neck. But I wasn't entirely ignorant of the events of that long-ago night before I was born. While my dad and mom never spoke directly to us about what happened inside that house in the woods, Molly and I grew up hearing stories that originated from both kids and adults about the boogeyman who resided there. How he killed a lot of people. How he killed his family. I never really believed the stories until that one day thirty years ago when Molly and I came face-to-face with the boogeyman himself.

"Your father arrested the fourteen-year-old boy on the spot," Caroline went on. "He was convicted and because of his age, treated as a youth. A 'crime of passion' they called it—the desperate action of an abused youth. In the end he was incarcerated for ten years in a mental institution just outside of Saranac. By the time he was released in 1973, he was twenty-four years old. He returned to that house that by now was surrounded by thick woods. Joseph kept to himself, but we were still acutely aware of his presence. It was as if the devil himself was in our midst.

"Then women started going missing. Young women, some of them girls. No one attributed their disappearance to him at first, but I think your father suspected. Finally, an Albany woman had the guts to come forward and identify Whalen in a lineup. He'd abducted and attempted to rape her, but somehow she'd managed to get away. After she came forward so did a few others who'd been lucky enough to escape him.

"They sent him away then for thirty years and what we thought would be for good. You girls were still young at the time so I can't begin to describe the sigh of relief that was breathed by our entire community."

I took in Caroline's story. Each one of her words seemed to bear a great weight. I had no idea about my father, about what he'd seen, about what he'd been ordered to do by his state trooper superiors. In my mind I pictured him walking up the stairs of that horrible house to witness the dead bodies. I knew then without a shred of doubt that the reason he forbade me and Molly to enter those woods had not so much to do with a stream that ran as deep and strong as a river or the cliff and waterfall beyond it.

It had everything to do with Whalen. The boogeyman. Molly and I had always known that the monster was the real reason for Trooper Dan insisting we keep out of those woods. But to us, the monster didn't seem quite real. He seemed made up. The stuff kids and some adults with a sick sense of humor tell you in order to scare you. It wasn't until that monster stole us away and dragged us into that basement that we became aware of the real evil that existed in those woods. And once we escaped it, Molly and I made a pact to never tell a soul. To never tell anyone for fear the boogeyman would come back and this time kill our mom and dad.

Later on, when Molly and I had heard the news about Whalen's rape conviction and that he would be sent to prison for a time that seemed forever, we felt a sense of calm wash over us. We felt secure because he wouldn't be able to get to us from prison. He wouldn't be able to hurt us or our parents.

Caroline stood.

"Joseph Whalen," I said, my voice stuttering, stammering, eyes tearing. "When Molly and I were twelve…" She pressed her open hand against mine. "We…never…told anyone."

She too began to cry. "I know," she said, patting my hand. "I didn't always know. But now after what happened to you in the woods on Friday…after what the detective told me. But what I don't know, Rebecca, is the whole story."

I inhaled a deep breath and exhaled. Then I proceeded to tell Caroline everything about what happened to Molly and me in the woods thirty years ago, just like I'd revealed it to Michael only a couple of days earlier. When I was through with the story, Caroline didn't say a single word. Together we washed ourselves in a silence so thick and weighted, it seemed it could never be broken.

Until Franny came back in.

Chapter 77

HE HAD A SMILE ON HIS ROUND FACE. I DIDN'T KNOW whether to attribute the smile to the pie he'd just eaten inside the hospital cafeteria or to the painting he was about to give me.

The final painting.

As he picked it up and brought it to my bed, I felt my heart beat. In my head, flashes of images. Faces. Michael. Molly. Whalen.

Like the other four before it, this image took my breath away. Unlike the others, however, it did not frighten me. What this image represented was the end of something.

It was an almost exact representation of Molly and me. We were sitting by the stream in the woods, still dressed in our cut-off jeans and T-shirts. Molly was washing me with the stream water, washing my hair, washing me with the cold, clean water and her gentle hand. It had been only moments since Whalen had attempted to do terrible things to us and failed. But now he was gone and Molly was being strong. Strong enough for the both of us. Molly was washing me in the stream. It was a baptismal ceremony: Molly making all things new again.

I laid my head back on the bed, into the soft pillow. I wanted to cry. For Molly, for Michael, for Franny, for everyone. But I felt that I couldn't possibly cry another tear.

This painting was the end of something.

Somehow I was happy about that. Happy and sad at the same time.

"What's its title, Franny?" I asked, already knowing the answer.

"*Touch,*" he said softly.

Molly *touching* me as she washed away Whalen's horror. His evil.

Maybe there were no more tears to shed, but I felt myself choking up. I felt my heart and my lungs and all my organs twist inside out. "You were there, weren't you?" I said. "All those years ago in the woods. You saw what happened to Molly and me. You must have seen it all through a basement window."

He stood by the bed in his baggy jeans and yellow suspenders and he did something that was so rare for an autistic man: he began to cry. He cried for the both of us. It was all too true. Franny had witnessed the attacks and couldn't find a way to express what he'd seen. He couldn't communicate it until now, this very week. Like me, like Molly, Franny had been carrying the burden for nearly his entire life.

He must have known that Whalen had been freed. He must have used his special extrasensory gifts to intuit Whalen's intent— the intent to come after me. Franny sensed the danger and he tried to warn me through his art, his special language. He tried to save my life even before it required saving.

Chapter 78

THE NURSE CAME BACK IN WITH MY LUNCH, WHICH she set down on the table beside me. I couldn't bear the thought of eating. Attached to the nurse's clipboard was a strip of paper. She pulled the piece of paper off the board and held it in her hand. Just a small strip of litmus paper about the size of a cigarette, its tail end painted with pink.

When the nurse glanced at Caroline, I could only assume that she took her for my mother, and Franny for my brother.

"I have some good news, Rebecca," she announced. "You're going to have a baby."

For some reason I could not explain, the news didn't throw me into the least bit of shock. The effect it had was good and kind. It made me feel warm inside; it made me feel healed.

Caroline came to me, hugged me without getting in the way of the wires. "From out of the bad comes the good," she whispered in my ear. "Where there is death, there is life."

I believed her.

In my mind I'd thought about all the people I'd had relations with over the past many months. The past many years.

Michael. He was the only one.

I pictured him doing what he loved—working at his laptop, biting the nail. I saw him sitting at a small table sipping cappuccino outside a Paris café; I saw him working at a desk inside a New York City hotel room. I felt him lying beside me in bed, our bare feet touching.

Michael, don't die.

Chapter 79

MICHAEL WAS BEING KEPT ALIVE INSIDE A CLEAR, partitioned room in the ICU. Caroline wheeled me into the dimly lit room, pushing me to the bed that held my ex-husband's comatose body. When Caroline left the room, I took Michael's hand in mine. Already it felt cold and as frail as Molly's had just before she died all those years ago.

There was an IV attached to his left forearm by means of a needle and clear plastic tubing. The monitors set beside the bed recorded blood pressure and heart rate.

Although dark hair veiled more than half his face, I could see just how pale he was.

"We're going to have a baby," I whispered. "How about that? A couple of divorcees starting a family together."

I squeezed cold fingers together and I began to cry. For a brief second, Michael's eyes opened up. I felt my heart race. But just like that, his eyes closed and a short breath escaped his mouth.

That's when the green line on the monitor went flat and an electronic alarm sounded.

"I'm sorry," I cried. "I'm sorry we ever left one another, Michael."

A nurse came in then. She didn't look at me at all. She approached the machine and turned off the alarm. Glancing down at her wristwatch, she made a mental note of the time.

Before walking back out, she set her hand on my right shoulder and gently squeezed.

"Stay with him for a bit," she said.

She closed the door behind her.

I stayed with Michael for a while. I cried and I also talked to him, planned things out. I even told him about Robyn, how she was also going to have a baby. But after a time I knew it was no use. Michael had waited to die until I came to him one last time. Until I said good-bye.

Michael waited to die. He loved me that much.

I let go of his hand knowing I would never hold it again. I let go of his hand. But still I felt it in mine.

Michael.

I let go of his hand. It was time to let him go.

Chapter 80

ONE WEEK LATER I RECEIVED MY DISCHARGE. MY doctor's healing instructions in hand along with a big fat bill (the Albany Art Center couldn't afford comprehensive health care), I packed up my bag with *get well* cards, sympathy cards, and gifts and tossed out the now-wilted flowers. Then I wrapped Franny's final *Touch* painting in aluminum foil that one of the nurses had snatched up from the floor kitchen. Everything set to go, I settled into an Albany Medical Center wheelchair.

I'd lost five pounds over the past week, but the weight loss didn't make me feel any lighter. Nor was it good news for my pregnancy. Michael's parents were still alive, but in their mind I was still his wife and they saw to it to wait on burying him until I was well enough to attend the funeral. But I was no longer his wife, even if I was the mother of his unborn baby. Only when the funeral was over would I share the news about my pregnancy with Michael's parents.

I shared an elevator with Caroline and Franny.

Staring straight ahead, I caught my reflection in the chrome-paneled doors. My black-and-blued face stared back at me, distorted, unfamiliar, like a beat-up funhouse mirror reflection.

Almost tranquilly the elevator descended three stories to the first floor where we proceeded along the extended length of the narrow corridor to the exit. Franny and I were barely through the automatic sliding glass doors before scattered reporters besieged us with questions regarding our overnight ordeal of one week ago.

"Is it true Whalen abducted you and your twin sister thirty years ago?"

"Do you fear for your life now that Whalen's body has yet to be located?"

The questions were machine-gunned as microphones were shoved to within inches of our faces while we made for the parking lot.

Until Caroline took control.

She stopped the chair, stepped around to the front, blocking any and all access to Franny and me.

"Ladies and gentlemen," she exclaimed. "Please leave us in peace. In time, we'll release a statement regarding last week's ordeal. But until then we ask for patience and understanding while the process of convalescence continues. Thank you."

As soon as I was seated beside Franny in the front of Caroline's old truck, I decided to break my silence. "That was eloquent, Caroline," I offered, eyes planted on the open road up ahead.

Throwing the automatic transmission into drive, she said, "I've had a lifetime of protecting Francis from vultures like that."

For a moment I was reminded of Franny's upcoming cable television debut. But I thought better of mentioning it now.

While she motored the truck past the city limits, over the South Troy Bridge and along Rural Route 2, Caroline brought me up to speed on a few developments that had transpired over the past twenty-four hours.

First, Robyn had been transported to her mother's home in the Albany suburbs where she continued to recover. Silently, I brooded over my best friend and partner not having called or come to visit me. But then, I knew something about post-traumatic stress. I knew about wounds that change a person, make them withdraw—wounds that even time couldn't heal. Caroline went on to say that the FBI still had no clue as to the whereabouts of Robyn's attacker, and in all likelihood would not until someone either caught him in the act, or make a positive ID in a line-up.

The next item was very important: it was believed that traces of Whalen's body were uncovered in the deep woods not far from Mount Desolation. Specifically recovered were several bones that might belong to his right hand. Not even the press was aware of the discovery since the remains were now arriving at the FBI forensics lab in Albany for DNA verification.

"Is Mr. Whalen dead now?" Franny asked, his eyes staring out the windshield onto the pine tree–lined road.

I took hold of his hand, squeezed it, but then quickly released it. "Yes Franny," I said. "You don't have to worry."

"What if he's not dead? Does Mr. Whalen come back for us?"

I'm not sure if it was a conscious move, but Caroline tossed me a tight-lipped glance. I knew what she was thinking without her having to say it. That all DNA tests aside, until Whalen's entire body was uncovered, she would not believe he was dead.

Neither would I.

I spent another full week at the Scaramuzzis' farm recovering from my wounds. Exactly two weeks to the day after he was attacked, Michael's body was released for burial. It took some effort, but as a part of his eulogy I read a few pages from *The Hounds of Heaven* and it didn't surprise me one bit that not a dry eye could be found inside St. Pious Church—the same church where we buried Molly and my parents all those years ago.

After the church ceremony, I rode to the cemetery in the front seat of Caroline's truck (Franny was allowed to stay home and paint by himself). While a handful of us surrounded the gravesite, the priest said a few more prayers on Michael's behalf. The day was cold and blustery. When we set red roses on his casket, the red petals shivered in the wind gusts.

As the service came to an end and everyone scattered away from the grave, I stood alone with my ex-husband. I told him I loved him. I thanked him for what we had during the final week of our lives together. I set a hand on my belly, told him I'd take care of our son for us. I didn't know for certain I was going to have a boy, but whenever I tried to picture the baby inside of me, I saw a little Michael.

While Caroline stood waiting for me by the open door of her truck, I felt my ex-husband's loss like a person might feel a limb that has suddenly been amputated. "I'm sorry we ever left one another," I said, brushing away a tear from my eye. "I will always love you, and I will tell him all about his father and what a great writer he was and an even greater husband and friend."

When I walked away from the grave, I didn't feel like I was leaving Michael behind. I felt as though he were walking right beside me and our baby. I felt his presence that strongly. And because he would be with me always, I knew it would be a long time before I returned to the cemetery.

Chapter 81

CAROLINE AND I DIDN'T SAY A WHOLE LOT ON THE WAY back across the river to Rensselaer County. I had assumed we'd drive straight to her house for the small reception she was putting on for those who'd attended the funeral. Instead we took the long way around the backside of Mount Desolation. When she pulled off the main road onto an overgrown two-track, I turned to her.

"Where are you taking us?"

"Closure." She smiled, as the truck shook and lumbered to and fro. "I can't think of a better place for it to happen."

The two-track was hardly even a two-track anymore, it was covered with so much growth. We must have driven two miles before we could go no further. Not without getting the truck caught up on some heavy rocks that blocked the parallel tracks. Obstacles no doubt placed there by the boogeyman himself.

Caroline got out. "We walk from here," she said.

"But what about Whalen, Caroline?" I said, feeling my pulse speed up at the thought of exiting the truck.

Caroline didn't answer right away. Instead she reached into her purse and pulled something out. It was a pistol. A chrome-plated six-shot revolver like my dad used to carry as his back-up weapon when he was still a state trooper.

"I don't expect even a monster like Whalen to return to the scene of his most recent crime, even if he is still alive. But if he happens to show his face, I'll be happy to blow it to smithereens for him."

Setting the gun onto her lap, she then reached into my purse.

"I'm doing this for you," she said, her eyes locked onto mine. When she pulled out my old copy of *Mockingbird*, I had no idea what she had in store for it. Nor did I ask as we slipped out of the truck. When I saw her reaching into the truck's cargo bed, where she picked up an old metal gasoline can imprinted with a yellow-and-black Sunoco logo, I asked her what she thought she was doing.

She looked at me from across the expanse of the pickup bed.

"I'm going to burn the place," she said. "I'm going to burn the house along with your memories of Whalen."

I thought about all the hours I'd spent drawing the boogeyman's face in the margins of that book. I thought of all the years I'd been carrying it around with me as a reminder of something I so badly wanted to forget. If that makes any kind of sense at all. Maybe Caroline was right. We should burn the place down. Burn my book. Kill the mockingbird for real.

I felt the presence of the baby growing in my tummy. I thought about Robyn's baby, too. And I thought about Michael. If he were with me at that very moment, he would have taken hold of my hand and squeezed it. It would have been an affirmation that sometimes, the past should not only be forgotten, it should be destroyed. Caroline was right. Maybe it was time I destroyed the past in order to move on with my life.

"If we burn the place," I said, "what happens to the police investigation? Won't everything be destroyed? The evidence that will be used against Whalen?"

"Whalen, if he is still alive, is his own worst evidence," she said. "Besides, these woods contain the bodies of the missing women he abducted, raped, and killed. That's the real evidence."

I nodded at her, as if to say, *Let's do it.*

"Let's go," she ordered, that same subtle smile painted on her face.

To some of the animals watching from their hideaway dens, we must have been some kind of sight. Two grown women, dressed all in black, making their way through the woods, one of them still sporting a heavy cast on her right hand. I almost felt like laughing. Instead I just kept quiet and followed Caroline for the ten-minute walk into the dark woods.

I'd never before come upon the front of the old Whalen house. I'd always approached it from the backside. As we emerged from the woods, I felt that familiar pressure in the stomach—the organ slide in my intestines. My eyes gazed upon the warped and mold-covered roof shingles, the gray-brown siding, the decayed and now completely detached front porch. I eyed the picture window, the glass now shattered and leaving only jagged edges. I imagined that at one time it would have offered a view of a front lawn, two little children playing on it. A boy and a little girl. I imagined a mother looking out the window onto the children, maybe while she dusted the furniture, while a stew or maybe a chicken was cooking in the kitchen.

But then I pictured that boy having grown into a teenager. I pictured him walking into the house late one night, a shotgun in his hand. I saw that boy moving methodically from bedroom to bedroom until his horrific deed was done.

Without a word Caroline stepped onto what was left of the front porch that now was wrapped with yellow ribbon bearing the words, CRIME SCENE: KEEP OUT. With gas can and my old novel in hand and pistol tucked into the waist of her jeans, she raised her right leg like a woman thirty years younger, and kicked the door in. Proceeding under the police "crime scene" plastic ribbon, she entered into the place and disappeared. Maybe three long minutes later, she reemerged with that old Sunoco gas can in her hand, the metal canister appearing far lighter than it had been before she'd entered the house. Setting the can onto the porch floor, she pulled something from the pocket of her black pants.

A book of matches.

Striking the match, she set the entire book on fire and tossed it into the open front door. Casually, as if she'd only set a bundle of red roses on the porch floor, she picked up the can and made her way back to me. By the time she reached me, the fire was already visible through the open door. Moments after that, the entire first floor caught fire.

It didn't take long for the whole place to go up in flames. I felt the heat on my face and I eyed the bright orange fire and I felt my hatred and fear melt out of my pores like candle wax.

Taking hold of my hand, Caroline kissed me gently on the cheek, setting an open hand on my belly.

"We should get back to Franny," she said. "He'll be worried."

Even though burning that house was entirely illegal, I already felt a great weight being lifted from my shoulders. I shot a glance up at the sky visible through the tops of the trees. I tried to picture Molly looking down on the scene, issuing a heartfelt thumbs-up.

"Way to fucking go, ladies!" she'd shout out.

Lowering my head, I turned away from the inferno, and never looked back.

Chapter 82

THE NEXT MORNING, I WOKE UP INSIDE MY APARTMENT alone. It was the first night I'd spent there since the events of the past few weeks had transpired—since Michael died. With Whalen still at large, I didn't sleep very well that first night, even with Michael's beret stuffed under my pillow to offer me a semblance of security, however false.

With Michael gone and with Robyn eyeing a far longer emotional recovery than her physical wounds would ever require, I had some serious decisions to make.

Would I go back to my teaching job at the art center? Would I continue to live in this apartment? Would I sell off my parents' house and the acreage that went with it? Would I move away from Albany? Maybe make the forever-dreamed-about move to New York City? Would I ever return to my art?

One thing was certain: I had a baby to think about now. Where to raise him and how to raise him would be of prime concern, which pretty much meant that my NYC residency might have to be put on hold once again.

No one should raise a child in the city, Michael used to say. *Unless they're filthy rich.*

I can't say that I disagreed with him. And he was still the baby's father, no matter what.

First things first, I jumped back into my routine. I made the coffee, poured a glass of juice, and took my vitamins, which now included prescription prenatals.

I poured a small bowl of shredded wheat and two-percent milk. When that small meal proved not to cut the mustard (I was eating for two now), I took advantage of Caroline and Franny's having kindly stocked my fridge and shelves with food. I got the frying pan out and lit the gas stove. Setting my open hand on my growing belly, I realized how famished I truly was.

I set out to make a big breakfast.

First I cracked two eggs into a bowl, beat them smooth along with a dab of milk, some salt and pepper. Then I added a teaspoon of salted butter to the pan. With the butter fully melted, I added the blended eggs into the pan, cooking the mixture slowly over a medium flame.

When the eggs were lightly cooked some two minutes later, I slid them out of the pan onto a white dinner plate. In the fridge I dug out some Green Mountain salsa and some grated Munster. Using my fingers I spread some of the cheese onto the steaming eggs. Last, but not least, a big glass of OJ on ice. I was so famished that I ate the food right there, standing inside the kitchen.

I was setting the dishes into the sink when the buzzer sounded. It wasn't unusual for the maintenance crew to be making inspections of one kind or another, especially on a Monday morning. But instead of buzzing the person in, I reminded myself of a free Whalen, and made the cautious decision to make my way out my front apartment door and up the steps to the door of my building. Through the glass I spotted a man wearing a FedEx uniform, behind him the still running, orange-on-white FedEx van. The man held a clipboard in one hand and a small package in the other.

The package was a standard eight-and-one-half-by-eleven envelope. I couldn't imagine what anyone wanted to send me that was so important that it had to arrive via FedEx. But I signed for it anyway, and took the package with me back inside the apartment.

In the kitchen, I tore the envelope open and peered inside. There was a photograph that was paper-clipped to a letter. Pulling the letter out, I could see that it was a handwritten note from Detective Harris. The attached photo was the black-and-white shot of Molly and me, the same one to be further examined by print specialists in Albany. The note was a simple one.

It said:

Dear Rebecca,

Whalen's prints were nowhere to be found on this picture. Neither are Francis Scaramuzzi's. Still awaiting results from Albany regarding bone samples taken from woods around Mount Desolation.

Take care of yourself,
Harris

So that was it, then.

Neither Whalen nor Franny had been in possession of the photo after all. I could only guess how it had gotten onto the front porch of my parents' house. If Whalen or Franny hadn't placed it there, then who had?

Exhaling a breath, I stuck the photo onto the fridge with a magnet. It was the only photograph that occupied the fridge. Tossing the FedEx envelope away, I grabbed my new cell phone, bringing it with me into the bathroom where I set it down onto the edge of the sink. I started the shower, letting the water warm up and the bathroom fill with steam. Although I had no definite plans, I would start the day by paying a visit to Robyn. We hadn't spoken since before Michael's death, and I suddenly found myself missing her like crazy.

Inside the bedroom, I took my pajamas off.

Standing before the Ikea body-length mirror, I stared at my stomach. Maybe I was only a little more than a couple of weeks along, but I swear I was beginning to show the first signs of a belly. It made me feel good to know that the baby was inside me, growing. Soon I wouldn't be alone. Soon I would have all the companionship I needed. It would come in the form of a small bundle of joy.

I made my way back into the kitchen, where I placed a plastic shopping bag over my cast-covered right hand and secured it with a rubber band from out of the junk drawer. In the bathroom, I pulled back the curtain and carefully stepped into the hot shower. It was the first shower I'd taken inside my own bathroom in what felt like ages. I felt the good, hot water wash over my skin. I felt it seep *under* my skin. I felt it heal the many wounds I'd received up on that mountain and down inside the stone basement of that house in the woods.

The house that no longer existed.

I let the water pour over my hair and onto my face. I felt the good feel of the hot sting. I poured shampoo onto my hair, kneaded it in with my uninjured hand. The thick foam ran down my face. When a little got into my eyes I felt the sting, but I didn't mind. I actually started to laugh, as though getting soap in your eyes was the funniest thing in the world. I'm sure it was just the joy of being alive, being pregnant with a child I really wanted and really looked forward to loving. It would be my purist work of art.

Placing my face directly below the nozzle, I let the water spray directly into my eyes until the sting started to go away. I kept my eyes closed tightly while I rinsed my hair. When the cell phone chimed, I automatically whispered, "Crap." Of course someone *had* to be calling me while I took a shower, while I was blinded by soap in my eyes. I immediately thought of Robyn. Her beautiful face flashed through my mind. Not the damaged one I witnessed in the Albany Medical ICU, but the one I looked forward to seeing every day at the School of Art. Was my best friend finally making contact? I might have simply waited until my shower was over to check and see, but I couldn't help myself. Reaching outside the shower curtain, I picked the cell phone up off the sink, opened it to see that a new text had been delivered.

I opened the message.

Cry, cry, cry, little kitten.

The bathroom door shot open, slamming against the tile wall. The shower curtain flew open, revealing the swelled, bruised face of the boogeyman. His hand shot out and wrapped itself around my throat. I dropped the cell into the tub. The hand choked me. Cut off all my air. I reached out for him. Tried to claw him. Claw his face. But all I could grab onto was plastic curtain. The hot shower rained down on me while the curtain began to tear away from the rod, one ring at a time. The pop-popping noise of the breaking plastic filled the bathroom along with shower spray, along with my muted gasps, along with Whalen's high-pitched moans.

Stepping into the tub, Whalen revealed a knife gripped in his left hand. He pressed the blade of the knife up against the lower portion of my neck, just under his other hand that was choking me. He quickly pulled the knife back an inch or two, cutting into my skin. The pain shot up and down my spine. I wanted to scream, but he was choking me.

My vision escaped me. I saw blackness lit up with stars, neurons exploding in my brain.

He pressed the knife up against the underside of my ribcage. He pressed the sharp blade up against my skin, flicked the knife back quick.

More burning pain.

My legs went wobbly. Blood poured down my ribs and belly.

Then an explosion. A gunshot.

The hand that choked my neck released and fell away. The knife dropped into the tub. I looked down, saw the blood circling the drain, circling the thin knife and my shattered cell phone. Whalen's body fell back out of the tub, and hit the tile floor hard. I heard footsteps. Out the corner of my eyes, I saw the blurry image of Detective Harris. In his right hand he held an automatic. He grabbed the towel from the rack, put it into my hands.

I was too shocked, too frightened to speak, to cry, to do anything but cover myself up.

"How bad are you hurt?" he demanded.

I managed to shake my head while I got my air back.

He reached down with his right hand, pressed two fingers against Whalen's jugular.

"He's gone."

My back pressed up against the slick ceramic wall, I sank down into the tub, the water spray shooting down onto my head, onto my now exposed cast.

Whalen was gone.

I shivered and was suddenly overcome with the urge to cry.

Cry, cry, cry…

It's exactly what I did.

Chapter 83

MORE POLICE CAME. SO DID STATE TROOPERS, WHO blocked off the entrance to the apartment complex with their blue-and-yellow cruisers.

The EMTs came. The press showed up. TV *and* print.

Caroline and Franny rushed to the scene when they got wind of it on the radio.

I sat in the back seat of Harris's Jeep. He'd sent one of the uniformed officers out for tea and I now held a steaming cup in my trembling hands. The EMTs had already looked me over, examined the wounds to my neck and chest. The surface cuts required no stitches. Only butterfly bandages. As for my neck, I'd sustained some bruising, but no permanent damage. Still, they insisted I be transported immediately to the hospital for further tests and observations. Given the condition of my healing heart along with the early stage pregnancy, there was no telling what I might suffer in the short term.

I flat out refused.

I'd just been released from the hospital two weeks before. Tests had proved there had been no permanent damage to my heart after having suffered the mild heart attack up on Mount Desolation. The EMTs looked at me with skeptical frowns. They asked me to sign a waiver of release absolving them of any and all responsibility should I drop dead on the spot. I did it.

Then they left me alone.

As soon as Whalen's body was bagged and lifted into the back of a big, black SUV with tinted windows, Harris joined me in the Jeep. He sat behind the wheel, an identical Styrofoam cup in his hand, the only difference being his held black coffee.

He asked me if I was all right. I sipped my tea, running the exposed fingers on my damp, cast-covered right hand through my still wet hair and breathed.

"Just a little shaken up is all."

He sipped his coffee. "You know that now, without question, Whalen is out of your life forever," he consoled. "Without…question."

"The future is bright," I joked with a wry smile. But I immediately stared back down into my tea as the smile once more became a frown. "How did you know Whalen would be here?"

"I didn't, really. Late last night I got a call from forensics in Albany telling me the bones found on Mount Desolation didn't belong to a male matching Whalen's age and characteristics. In fact, the bones probably belonged to a female who passed away decades ago. More than likely, one of Whalen's early abduction victims.

"Our theory now is that he buried the women outside his home in the woods and periodically re-interred them, laying them to rest in different areas in and around Mount Desolation, until finally laying them to rest down inside that basement *after* he was released from prison. That would explain why we never uncovered remains inside his house all those years ago. It's not that he was always one step ahead of us. It's just that we just didn't have the technology we have at our disposal nowadays.

"All morning long I thought about it. If the bones didn't belong to Whalen, there was a good chance he'd survived the damage inflicted to his head by Francis. Which meant he might still be out there, waiting to strike again."

"What about the black-and-white photo you returned to me along with a note?"

He shook his head, vehemently. "I jumped the gun when I sent that out yesterday afternoon. It dawned on me that Whalen's prints didn't have to be on that photograph for it to have been in his recent possession. The man spent thirty years in prison. It's possible he slowly but surely scraped away the prints on his fingers. Anyone can do it with a common household disposable razor blade."

"But wouldn't the parole officers pick up on that?" I asked. "Fingers with no prints?"

He nodded. "Good point. But even if he had left his fingerprints on the picture, it's not impossible for him to dissolve them from the picture's face before planting it on your folk's porch floor."

"And the jimmied window? That was Whalen?"

"I can only imagine that he wanted to get a personal feel for your childhood home. You know, step into the footsteps of his beloved Molly and Rebecca, his two little kittens. I now believe he broke into the home many times over the past six months. He scoured the place and came up with the photo. On the day you went out to Brunswick to have a face-to-face with Caroline Scaramuzzi, Whalen followed you and planted the pic in a spot where you'd be likely to find it. Another way of playing with your head."

"But how did Franny paint that exact image of us back in the seventies if he never had access to the photo?"

"That's just it," Harris said. "He did have access to it. In fact, dozens of people did."

I didn't quite understand what he was getting at, until he reached into the Jeep's glove box, pulled something out. "Caroline gave this to me yesterday after I'd already FedExed the original to you."

He handed it to me.

It was a Christmas card. A postcard-sized Christmas card with a reproduction of that same black-and-white photo of Molly and me printed beside the words "Happy Holidays." Written in my mother's unmistakable ballpoint, "Merry Christmas and Happy New Year from the Underhills." It was dated December 3, 1976. I remember how excited my mother was that year to discover that for a few dollars, the photo lab could make post-cards out of a common black-and-white snapshot. That was the reason Franny was able to paint Molly and me all those years ago.

"But how did you know Whalen was coming back for me here at my apartment? How did you know he was going to do it today?"

"Intuition, plus a little help from your friends, the Scaramuzzis."

I shook my head, not comprehending him.

"Caroline called me on my cell as soon as you left her house last evening. She didn't want you to know that she called me. But she felt it would be the prudent thing to do, considering Whalen hadn't been officially declared dead yet and this was the first night you'd be alone since the incident on the mountain.

"I acted on a hunch. Instead of going home last night, I parked outside your apartment. When the FedEx truck pulled up to your building I took notice of a strange-looking individual walking around the back toward your terrace door. He was dressed in blue overalls like a maintenance man. I didn't like the looks of it.

I followed him, right into the apartment." He took another sip of coffee. "The rest you know."

I sat back, felt my hands, warm around the cup of tea. "I never knew," I exhaled. "Never had a clue you were out there."

"I guess I've still got the touch." He grinned. "Maybe I'll go private when retirement kicks in."

"By the looks of it, you're only a few Xs away."

It was over. Finally. No more Whalen. Still, I didn't feel as relieved as I should have felt. Maybe relief would come when the events of the morning finally settled in. Who knew how long that would take?

Harris got out and was about to turn away when I stopped him.

"Detective," I said out the open window. "What about the cell phones? Had Whalen been stealing them from the Hollywood Car Wash like we thought?"

He nodded. "Stealing them, but not enough of them to make it seem too suspicious. Some of them are armed with codes that only the owners would know. Those phones would have been useless to him. But some of them, like yours, Rebecca, wouldn't be blocked by code. Those were the ones he'd go after. From what the manager told me, four or five phones were reported missing by various customers over a period of about six months. When you consider that the manager gets calls on a daily basis about a missing this or a missing that, he never would have suspected a pattern."

"Until you pointed it out to him."

"Exactly. In any case, it certainly explains how Whalen texted you without having to acquire his own cell phone account."

I took in a breath.

"Thank you, Detective." I smiled.

Harris left me alone again, and made his way back into the apartment.

I sat in the back seat, stared out onto the apartment parking lot and all the people that had gathered there. I looked at the scene for a full minute or two until the people began to disperse along with the police and the EMTs. I sat there in silence and looked until all that was left were Franny and Caroline against a backdrop of ivy-covered brick buildings. I'd left them standing there long enough. I got out of the Jeep and joined them.

When Harris came back to the Jeep, he nodded politely at Caroline and Franny, then told me he had to get back downtown.

I gave him a hug. "Thank you again," I said.

"Thank you for being strong," he said. "For all these years."

I looked into his eyes. "You never told me that you knew my father," I added.

He cocked his head. "I knew all about what your dad discovered in that house in the woods back in '63. I figured if he never told you, and you had never found out about it on your own, then why should I be the one to do it. By the looks of it, your father didn't want you to know. He wanted to protect you, Rebecca. You and Molly. He wanted to protect you from Whalen's evil."

He told me that he would be in touch. That he would need to question me further later on in the week.

With a smile on his face, he got back into the Jeep and took off.

I could only assume that for a man on the verge of retirement, he too had realized some serious closure this morning with Whalen's death—with having personally put a bullet in the monster, the devil, the boogeyman. I know I did. *But then why did I feel so sad about the apparent source of all those texts? Had I ever really believed that they'd somehow come from Molly? Was it possible I could believe in something heaven-sent?*

Standing in the parking lot, I faced my friends. "You guys want to come in?" I asked. "Get out of the cold?"

Franny smiled. It was a rare event to see him smile. It made me feel good to see it.

"We'll go inside your apartment," Caroline exclaimed. "It's a crime scene now. We'll pack up your things and move them back to the farm. *Our* farm."

I took a look back around at the apartment building. I pictured the torn-away shower curtain, the bloodstains, the yellow police ribbon that blocked off access to the bathroom. I would help Caroline pack my things. But I would never return to the place again, if I could help it.

Like Whalen, and that now burned-down house in the woods, it was all a part of the past. All that remained was to move on.

"Have you eaten?" Caroline asked.

"I had breakfast," I said, setting my hand on my stomach. "I'm not sure where I'm getting my appetite, but I could definitely eat again."

"Pancakes," Franny said, that smile still illuminating his round face. "Pancakes and blueberries and syrup."

I laughed.

Caroline laughed.

"Pancakes it is, Franny," I said. "I know a great little diner right around the corner."

Together the three of us made our way for Caroline's truck.

It seemed strange in a way. Only a little more than an hour before, I was about to be killed by a homicidal maniac. Now I was going out for pancakes. I recalled one of my mother's cherished sayings: God works in mysterious ways.

I looked up at the blue sky, smiled at Molly. I saw a patch of clouds and I swear I saw her face. In the clouds I made out Molly's face as though she were looking down at me and smiling. I might have been the only one to recognize the face. But it was there all the same. You just had to know how to look for it. Molly was in heaven, and she was watching out for me, for my life. Just as she always had.

There was no mystery in that.

TWO YEARS LATER

Chapter 84

DEAR MOL,

A lot has changed since I last wrote you.

After spending a year with the Scaramuzzis on their farm, I decided to move back into Mom and Trooper Dan's house. Robyn has moved in with me, and together we have started a private art school called, appropriately enough, the School of Art. We run it out of the house now. We have over fifty students, most of them young children. There are so many paintings, drawings, and sculptures hanging around that we also decided to renovate the barn and turn it into a gallery featuring the students' artwork. Franny himself contributed five pieces before he passed away in his sleep just before last Christmas. We were able to afford the barn's renovation with the sale of just one of those paintings. A quirky abstract on traditional landscape he called Listen.

After he appeared on MSNBC, the demand for his work quadrupled, along with the price per piece. Before he died, Franny had become a rock star before our very eyes. He saved my life and I will miss him with all my heart. I will never forget what he did for me, and for us. I will always love him.

Little Michael is walking now. He gets along so well with Robyn's little Molly that you would think they are brother and sister. Twins. They are inseparable and are permanent fixtures around the studio. Sometimes I like to think that you and Michael can see them from up in heaven. You would be so proud. Caroline has taken on the job of nanny. I wonder if one day we'll allow them to play flashlight tag behind the house. Naturally, the woods and Mount Desolation will be strictly forbidden territory.

Speaking of Robyn, the FBI finally caught up with her attacker. They found him inside a motel outside Chicago, where he was awaiting the arrival of his latest conquest. The FBI arranged a sting operation based upon some information delivered by a Match.com client who spotted a red flag when her new love interest insisted on meeting at a strange motel-no-tell. True to form, once he was caught, he couldn't resist bragging about his exploits all over the country, including a beautiful brunette in Albany, New York, by the name of Robyn. Robyn with a "y." Safe to say, the man will be put away for decades to come. God willing, he will spend his final days behind bars.

You'll be happy to know I'm painting again. Mostly landscapes. Nothing too difficult. Just enough to get the rust out. I've also decided to try my hand at completing Michael's final novel. Surprise of surprises, it's not a detective novel, but something entirely different. It's a story about a young woman who finds herself lost and alone in Europe. Paris, to be precise. When she meets another woman who is identical to herself in every physical sense, she discovers that her remembered past is far different from reality. In typical Michael fashion, he didn't leave me with a title. But for now I'm calling it Lost and Found.

I miss you, Mol.

I know you were with me on that night two years ago when Whalen made his final move. I know you were there because I felt your presence with every one of my five senses. I smelled your skin, I heard your voice, I felt your touch. You entered my body and gave me strength. You made me fight my fear. You helped me survive. You are never far from my thoughts, my memories, my dreams.

Sometimes when I wake up early in the morning, I go outside with my coffee and I look out over the field to the woods and the mountain. I still see you walking through the tall grass in your cut-off jeans and Paul McCartney and Wings T-shirt. I see your blonde hair bobbing in time with your every step. I still feel that little pang of fright in my stomach the closer we come to the woods. I don't know how our lives would have turned out had we not entered the woods that day, had we not broken Trooper Dan's rule. But I guess it's silly to imagine that we would have turned out any differently. We are what we are at any given moment in time. Dead or alive.

I'm going to end this now, because I hear Michael singing in his crib.

It's morning and I need to make the coffee before I get him out. I may not write you for a while. There're too many things I have to do now; too much life to live. Besides, I want to save up all the good juicy bits for when we meet up again, identical face to identical face. We'll have a lot of catching up to do. I'd like to say I can't wait, but it's probably going to be a while.

All my love.

Your twin sister,

Rebecca Rose Underhill

The End

ABOUT THE AUTHOR

VINCENT ZANDRI, TRAVELER, adventurer, foreign correspondent, and freelance photojournalist, is the international best-selling author of *The Innocent*, *Godchild*, *Moonlight Falls*, *Concrete Pearl*, *Scream Catcher*, as well as the digital shorts *Pathological* and *Moonlight Mafia*. An MFA in writing graduate of Vermont College, he lives in New York.